WILL YOU, WON'T YOU?

JESSIE HAAS

WILL YOU, WON'T YOU?

Greenwillow Books
An Imprint of HarperCollins*Publishers*

The quotations on pages 107–108, 110, and 157 are by Robert Burns
from the poems "To a Mouse" (1785) and "To a Louse" (1786).

The text of this book is set in Galliard.

Library of Congress Cataloging-in-Publication Data
Haas, Jessie.
Will you, won't you? / by Jessie Haas.
p.   cm.
"Greenwillow Books."
Summary: Spending the summer with her strong-willed
politician grandmother, fourteen-year-old Mad achieves
breakthroughs in both her horseback riding and her
Scottish dancing and begins to develop the
self-confidence she has always lacked.
ISBN 0-06-029196-6 (trade). ISBN 0-06-029197-4 (lib. bdg.)
[1. Self-confidence—Fiction. 2. Grandmothers—Fiction.
3. Dance—Fiction. 4. Horses—Fiction.
5. Politics, practical—Fiction.] I. Title
PZ7.H11133 Wi 2001   [Fic]—dc21   00-025382

1   2   3   4   5   6   7   8   9   10   First Edition

For the friends who teach me:

Susan Hirschman

Bernard McGrath

Senator Cheryl Rivers

Will you, won't you, will you, won't you, will you join the dance?

—From "The Lobster-Quadrille" in
Alice's Adventures in Wonderland by Lewis Carroll

1

WHEN TWO PEOPLE are packing everything but the furniture into suitcases and closets, getting ready to sublet the apartment and leave for the summer, accidents will happen.

Still, you don't expect to walk into the living room and find your mother reading your Language Arts diary.

She looked up, pink but not embarrassed. "So sue me!"

I just stood there, with my mouth open.

"If a diary is left on the coffee table," Mom said, "with a paragraph underlined and starred, some people would call that a cry for help!"

Not really. Mrs. Lum guaranteed she wouldn't read our pages, only count—

"Listen to this!" Mom addressed our unseen audience: the packed courthouse, the television cameras. Sometimes it's my father. L.G., he's called, for Long Gone, or G.R., for Good Riddance. " 'I have set a record—three consecutive school days without speaking a single word to anyone. No one meets my eye. I have actually become invisible!' "

I said, "It was an important achievement."

Her brows snapped together, and she looked down at the diary as if she couldn't stand not to turn the page and read on. "It's *true?* You *worked* at this?"

At times like this I hold on to two thoughts. One, most of me *is* invisible. I'm like a pipe in a nuclear plant, corroded from the inside. What looks like half-inch steel is really as thin as a credit card. *But nobody can see that!*

The other thought condenses into three words: attorney at law. That's my mom, the short, cute one, never more charming than when she's moving in for the kill. "Kitten," Judge Handry calls her, in defiance of all that's politically correct: a fluffy little fur ball toying expertly with a mouse.

I've seen mice get away by staying absolutely still.

"I thought school was better!"

"It was all right." And it was over! Even now my heart spiked with joy. No more middle school, ever again!

"*All right?* You *like* not talking to people?"

Yes. I like that. I like being unnoticed. When something interesting is going on, sometimes even *I* forget I'm there.

"*Now* what am I supposed to do?" Mom looked from the diary to the herd of suitcases huddled near the door. There was nothing she *could* do.

Tomorrow we'd put my cases in the leased truck, pick up the horse trailer and Cloud, and drive a hundred miles to Gam's house, where I'd spend the summer. Summer began yesterday, when I got my eighth-grade credits in, two weeks early. Mom would come back here for her suitcases, drive to the airport, and fly south to D.C. on a three-month job with the Justice Department.

"I'll be fine," I said. Uh-oh! Too smug.

Light flared in Mom's eyes. "Riding, reading, and *rotting*!"

"Hey—the Three Rs!"

"Hey *you*! You don't have to be me, you don't have to be your grandmother, but by God you're not turning into a mute psychotic on my watch!" She picked up the phone and punched the buttons with her thumb. Two rings. "Mother?"

There was a pause.

"I don't care if it's the attorney general, the governor, or God! Make it snappy! I need your help." She pressed the receiver button. "Do I *ever* call that woman when there *isn't* someone on the other line?"

I could have mentioned our own call waiting, the many times our own two lines are in play. But it wasn't the moment. "She just got home," I said. "She's probably exhausted."

The legislative session had dragged into mid-May, nearly ruining our plans. But a compromise tax cut had been worked out at two o'clock this afternoon. We'd last heard from Gam—"the powerful chair of the Senate Finance Committee"—on this evening's news, praising the bipartisan spirit of the legislature.

"If she has the energy to talk to the AG, she has the energy to talk to me!" Mom said.

When the phone rang ten minutes later, I was upstairs. The shower was running, but I was perched on the edge of Mom's bed. Half a ring. I heard from downstairs: "Mother?"

I eased the bedside phone out of its cradle and held it on my lap. Parker women have the kinds of voices that make speakerphones unnecessary.

"What is it, Ann?" Gam asked. "The short version. Jimmy's calling back in ten minutes." She sounded hoarse.

Mom sighed sharply. "I'll have a fight with you about your telephone manners tomorrow, Mother. Remind me! It's Mad."

"Mad what? What's wrong?"

"I'll read from her diary—and don't interrupt. We'll have that fight tomorrow, too. Listen: 'I have set a record—three consecutive school days without speaking a single word to anyone. No one meets my eye. I have actually become invisible!' "

Gam didn't respond for a moment. Then she asked, "Is it true?"

"What do you mean, is it true? Would she lie to her own diary?"

"If she thought her mother was going to read it, she might!"

"She doesn't deny it. She's proud of it! And she's set herself up a summer with no social life whatsoever. Who's she going to see at your place besides your political cronies? I don't like it. This is a bad age for girls."

My hand jumped to cover my mouth. I hate that phrase: a bad age. Like being told you're tired when what you are is angry. My problems don't have anything to do with the number of candles on my last birthday cake.

"What do you want from me?" Gam asked.

"Help me figure this out. Should I send her to a shrink? Summer camp? How can I make sure she socializes?"

Gam said, "I have an—darn!" The line went quiet for a moment.

"Ann, I've got to take this call, but don't worry. I know exactly what to do with Mad. She'll socialize all right! See y—"

"Wait, Mother! Is it raining there?"

"Raining? Of course it isn't raining!"

"Mad, you little *sneak*!" Mom's voice roared up the stairs and through the receiver at the same time. I dropped the phone, and from the floor Gam's laughter crackled.

I turned on the bed, drawing my feet under me. Mom came up the stairs two at a time and stood in the doorway, glaring. The shower made a shush of white noise in the background.

Gradually the brightness and danger dimmed out of Mom's face. Her shoulders sagged. "What are you turning into?" she whispered.

I couldn't answer. After a moment she went down the hall. The shower switched off. My heart did a quick thud. Turning *in*to? What am I turning *in*to?

Mom came back and slumped on the foot of the bed, staring off into space. "You were miserable," she said at last, in a voice that seemed to ache. "How could I not have seen that?"

"Well—" I pushed against the barrier in my throat. "I wasn't miserable at home."

"But why didn't you *tell* me?" She turned to me with tears glittering in her eyes. I looked down, pulling at a thread from the bedspread.

"What were you going to do? Beat them up?"

"Beat *who* up?"

I shrugged. "Oh, just—" Everybody, really. The boys who said "Mad Dog" in the hall, the ones who only snickered; the girls who made comments about my knees in the locker room, and the ones who pretended not to hear, and went on with their little cliques, and weren't Leslie . . . "Too big a job," I said. "Even for a Parker."

"Nothing's too big for a Parker. If I'd known it was that bad, I'd have sent you to Leslie's school. I'd have found a way!"

I didn't think so. Not with Cloud's board, my lessons, and 240,000 miles on the car. Besides, when Leslie's mother decided the middle school was "toxic" and sent her to private school after three months of seventh grade, Mom had a lot to say about making the public schools better, not abandoning them. She ran for the school board and got on the curriculum committee.

Curriculum wasn't my problem.

"It doesn't matter," I said. "It's over. Next year will be better."

"Why?"

"Leslie will be there."

"I see." She got up to pace between the bureau and the open suitcase. She prowls like this in court, thinking out a cross-examination.

At last she said, "I won't bother telling you, Mad, that you need more than one friend in life. I won't even mention that you might not have any classes with Leslie or that you might find new interests that would draw you away from each other."

"Thanks!" I said. "That's nice of you!"

Mom paused and pondered me. "You're *funny*," she said. "You make me laugh. I guess I thought you were that way in school, too. I thought you must be using it as a kind of armor. Not—*withdrawing*! Why didn't I hear one word about this? Why didn't one of those so-called counselors notice?"

Because I didn't want them to. I'd studied the herd, made myself notice the most unnoticeable kids, and copied them. It's not a mainstream look; for that you need bucks, because Kmart jeans are not okay. But you can get dark, baggy, worn-out clothes from the thrift shop very cheaply. Even if you don't actually have a tattoo or a piercing, you can look as if you might. The jocks and cheerleaders ignore you. The ones who really do have piercings seem to have other things to think about. I said, "I am good at it."

"Good at it? You're *good* at it?" Mom clutched her hair with both hands and, catching sight of herself as she swung past the mirror, stood and looked at her reflection. Slowly, without letting go of her hair, she turned. "I can't go to D.C. I'm not leaving you! It's Friday night. Who can I call?"

"Mom! This is crazy!"

"Crazy? You're turning yourself into a social anorectic—"

"It's just school!"

"Oh, yeah? Who do you talk to at the barn besides Leslie? Who else is your friend?"

"Jane," I said, at the same moment that she said, "Queen Jane doesn't count!"

We stared at each other. I could feel tears at the backs of my eyeballs. This was *way* out of control.

"You have to go," I said. "We can't stay here." People were coming to live in our apartment. Mom had a place already rented in Washington. The job was a big opportunity. "Listen, I'll just be at Gam's. I won't be seeing anybody anyway, so— I mean, I can't get any *worse*. You can straighten me out when you get back in September."

Slowly, slowly, Mom let go of her hair. "All right," she said. "All right. You make a point. We'll see what your grandmother has to say tomorrow."

And I'm not turning *in*to anything! I answered her, silently, in my room, with the door shut. I could hear her downstairs on the phone, but I wasn't even tempted to eavesdrop. I rolled up my pajama legs and looked at my knees.

The doctor calls it psoriasis, and until she started treatment, it didn't look bad—just patches where the skin turned silver and flaky, like the late stages of a scab. That was the summer after sixth grade, and I was used to having scabby knees.

But the doctor's ointment turned the patches red, and then came seventh grade. I didn't understand yet that in middle school someone is always looking at you, ready to pick you apart. I wore shorts for gym.

It might have been all right if I'd had lots of friends, but I didn't even have Leslie. Grades are divided alphabetically; Parker and Zebriski are a long way apart. No one else stood up for me. Even the nice kids were scared by middle school, or they'd changed.

So I was weird and ugly and alone. I had a disease that the doctor said was inherited, and it didn't come from Mom. L.G.'s legacy. I got sweatpants for gym, but it was too late.

Then Leslie's parents took her out of school, and I decided to turn invisible. Easier and safer than trying to make new friends. Practical. It helped. None of which I could explain to Mom or the Powerful Chair. They were going to punish me or cure me.

"Well, I don't care," I said aloud. I dropped the tube of ointment behind the bed. No more prescription refills! These legs are staying in blue jeans!

"Want to come check your e-mail?" Mom called from downstairs. "I'm about to put this thing in the closet."

```
from: lesismor@v.net
to: madwoman@v.net
subject: high school

Have you thought—I mean, really thought
about high school?
Because let's face it, I was a failure at
middle school.
I wimped out and had to be rescued.
Why won't that happen again? I need to
change this summer, but I don't know how—
Beyond we both need great new haircuts,
which we should do the week before school
starts, but . . .
It's four years! It's got to be better
than middle school, because my family
can't afford to rescue me again.
You stuck it out, Madwoman. Any ideas?
See you at the crack of freakin' dawn!
```

Click, click, click. The icons slowly faded, and the orange letters came up: IT IS NOW SAFE TO SHUT DOWN YOUR COMPUTER.

Good old e-mail! Leslie and I saw each other every day at the barn, but the truth came out afterward, on the screen. I'd always known Leslie thought I was tough, but I stayed in middle school only because I didn't have a choice. I couldn't say that. She was counting on me. I'd just have to *get* tough, as tough as she thought I was.

Well, I'd be spending the summer with the Queen of Tough. Maybe some of it would rub off!

"I know exactly what to do with Mad! She'll socialize all right!"

What could it be? I wondered as I helped Mom shove the computer into the hall closet. No matter what, it couldn't possibly be as bad as middle school!

2

NEXT MORNING at the barn Leslie and I didn't hug and cry. We are not huggers and criers.

We led Cloud out of her stall, crosstied her, and put on her maroon traveling blanket.

Then we knelt to put on the leg wraps. Leslie is small and dark and thin, with long, narrow eyes that seem secretive and can shut you out completely when she's upset. In her last days of middle school she was like that all the time, even in crowded hallways, especially in the cafeteria. I looked past her, into my empty, rumpled stall.

"I wonder who'll get it," Leslie said.

"As long as I get it back!" There's always a waiting list at Catamount Stables. Some lucky person would move in for the summer because I was leaving, would share our section of aisle, our crosstie, the stall frontage we decorated at Christmas and Halloween.

"I hope it's a horse Brando likes."

"I hope it's a guy," I said. "A cute guy, with a twin brother!" Front wraps on already; this was going much too quickly.

Leslie said, "As long as it's not one of the Club!" They were the girls who turned Catamount into a soap opera set. They had the best of everything from saddles to boot socks. They competed fiercely at hunter-jumper shows, made each other swear and cry and pressure their parents for ever more expensive horses, and they loved one another like sisters. So says Leslie, who has a sister.

They owned Club Row, the next aisle over. Leslie and I shared our aisle with two lawyers, an accountant, and a couple of computer analysts—and talked with them frequently, Mom! If Jane moved a Clubber here, the soap opera would follow. Nesta would go crazy. George might commit murder.

"Jane wouldn't do that," I said. "So, these haircuts—"

Beneath Cloud's belly, Leslie met my eyes. "Yeah. Well . . . I don't think haircuts are going to do it."

"You didn't wimp out," I said.

"Yeah, I did. I really did." Leslie stood up and leaned against Cloud's rump. I did the same.

"At least *you* can ride in shows!"

"That's not going to help me much in high school, Mad."

"Well . . . I don't know. Guts are guts, right?"

"Showing doesn't scare me, so I don't think that's guts," Leslie said. "Doing something you're scared of—like middle school—*that's* guts."

"I'd rather just not be scared," I said. Leslie only looked at me.

"Almost ready?" Mom stood at the end of the aisle, clutching her travel mug.

I turned away from Leslie. "I need my stuff from the tack room."

"Show me. I'll start loading."

I opened the door on the silent room full of saddles, pointed to my piles. Mom scooped up an armful, and I peeled off the note that was taped to my saddle cover.

3:00 A.M.

Dear Mad—

Sorry, no time to say much. Have to leave now or won't get to Oak Knoll in time for my first test.

Lovely chat with your mother at 9:30 P.M.

[Oh, *no!* I thought. Actual sweat popped out on my brow. Jane's lovely head hits the pillow at eight-thirty sharp. She gets up at four to feed, earlier when she's showing.]

So you're trying to become invisible? In which case why fall in love with a horse—admittedly, sweet, but lots of horses are sweet—whose whole life has been competition? Why work so hard to get good? Art for art's sake? Just trying to dope this out while my coffee drips.

Your mother wants me to make you show. You can lead a horse to water, I told her, etc. But you ought to think, Mad, if timid is what you want to be. We become what we practice. Think about it.

Have a great summer! Riding out in the open will help Cloud's impulsion; she's getting dull in the Indoor. You, too.

See you in September.

Jane

I folded the note three and then four times, creasing each fold with my thumbnail. I saw Jane in my mind's eye, blond and beautiful and athletic and perfect—what we all want to become, whether we have the genes for it or not.

Practice? Jane thought I was *practicing* timidity?

Why didn't she think I *was* timid? Why did she think I still had a choice?

"Mad? Almost ready?"

I stuffed the note in my pocket. Now, suddenly, we were really leaving. Cloud stepped into the trailer, we fastened the chains and the doors, checked all the lights, and Mom got behind the wheel. I stood by the open passenger door. "Hey."

"Hey," Leslie said.

"I'll e-mail you; we'll figure it out."

"Right."

"Well . . . see ya."

"See ya."

I climbed into the truck. In the side mirror I saw Leslie yawn and hug herself, smaller and smaller as we pulled away.

We traveled diagonally down our tiny state, from the highway to a wide paved road, a narrow paved road, a dirt road, and stopped beside the lilac bush, the bank of daylilies, and the battered mailbox that said PAR ER. "She still hasn't put the *k* back on," Mom said.

"Next campaign season."

Mom didn't even try to get the horse trailer into the yard. We let down the ramp and backed Cloud out onto the road. She looked around, calm and alert, her long white lashes winging across dark eyes—

"The grass is a foot high!" Mom said.

She was talking about the lawn, not the pasture, and she wasn't exaggerating. The brown remains of daffodils peeped over the fringe, and a flattened place showed where the rake had been left about a month ago.

The windows of the house looked blank and glossy, as if no one were home. But as I led Cloud up the drive, the side door opened. The Powerful Chair of the Senate Finance Committee, in a pink chenille bathrobe and flip-flops, stared at us speechlessly.

"Mother," Mom said, "have you had your coffee?"

Gam's lips parted like a desert traveler's.

"I'll be right in," Mom said, following me toward the barn.

I've always wanted to bring Cloud here, to this old barn with its cobwebs and junk-filled corners, the edges of boards rubbed soft by time and animals. I wanted her to spend a summer on pasture. I wanted to ride the trails and dirt roads Mom used to ride on her horse, Roxy, to go cross-country for hours and miles without ever making a circle or a figure eight, without ever passing a mirror.

I opened the stall door to see a meager hump of shavings in the middle of the floor. "Is that her idea of bedding? She didn't even spread it out!"

Mom found a rake and smoothed out the lump, and I led Cloud inside. Mom held her, I undressed her, and we stepped back to see how she'd take to her new surroundings. She made a brief tour, sniffing with a faraway look in her eye, stepped to the stall door, listened, sighed, and shoved her nose deep into the empty bucket.

"I'll leave you to settle her," Mom said, "and I'll go settle your grandmother."

I unclipped the bucket from its rusting snap. A spider ran frantically around the bottom. I dumped it onto the gravel and turned on the hose. The water smelled like molten rubber. I let it run, looking at the weeds, the tall grass, the paint peeling off the house.

I always felt a little sad here; it wasn't our home anymore, and Gamp was gone. Would I lose that sweet melancholy, living here for a whole summer?

Was I even staying? What were they talking about? I'd better get inside and find out.

The kitchen smelled like coffee. Gam bent over her mug, inhaling the steam. When she lifted her head, I almost jumped.

She had brown rings under her eyes, so large and deep you could have laid quarters in them. Her other wrinkles sagged to match. Her hair was flat on one side, pushed up on the other, and she sounded like a four-pack-a-day smoker. "Mad. Hi."

"Hi."

"I bought a bale of shavings, but it wasn't enough." She resorted to her coffee, lowering half the mug in two swallows. "We'll get more later."

"I'll do it," Mom said. She jiggled the toaster, and two pale slices popped up. Mom buttered them and put them in front of Gam, making space by pushing at the heap of mail that took up the center of the table. Envelopes and magazines slithered. The salt shaker was engulfed. Gam made a fence with her forearm to protect her breakfast and crunched wordlessly.

A newspaper clipping stuck out of my side of the mountain. I could see a date and a bit of headline: —KER SAYS. Geologically this was from the early Silurian Period, second week of the session. Parker says what? I pulled delicately. After a moment's resistance the clipping slid out.

SENATE ENGAGED IN SOCRATIC DIALOGUE, PARKER SAYS.

"The powerful chair of the Senate Finance Committee, responding to criticism—"

"Let me see that."

The Powerful Chair was on her feet, reaching over the heap for my clipping. Her political radar is always on. She turned the clipping, glanced at it, and her top lip pursed to a bitter point. "What swill!"

Mom and I glanced at each other. Gam believes in politics. She believes it's harmful and stupid to put down any part of the democratic process. Admittedly she believes that more at the beginning of the session than at the end, but still . . .

"Shower, Mother," Mom said. "We need to talk about Mad, and I want you rational."

Gam looked up from the clipping. "I told you. I know just what to do."

"And what is that?"

"Dance," Gam said. We both stared at her. "You remember my Scottish dancing. I told you about it, didn't I?"

Dancing? No! I thought. No! If there's anything worse than team sports—

"It's like square dance," Gam said. "I go to class once a week, and there are parties. There's one tonight, as a matter of fact."

Mom said, "Once a week do-si-doing with a bunch of senior citizens is not my idea of—"

Gam smacked her palm on the table. Coffee slopped onto the paper mountain. "Ann, *listen* for once in your life! You don't know what you're talking about! You've tuned out every word I ever told you about this, haven't you?"

Mom drew a long breath and held it a moment. I sat feeling the rapid, thready beat of my heart. A rabbit probably feels like this when it's pretty sure the fox has seen it.

"Yes," Mom said. "I've tuned you out. Go on."

Gam said. "It's about manners—"

"Her manners are fine!"

"*Are* they? How did that come about?"

They stared hard at each other. Mom looked down first. "I should know better than to take you on the day after a session!"

"Scottish country dancing," Gam said, "is about social distance: how you create it, how you maintain it, how you bridge it." Her voice began to expand. Her shoulders squared so she took up more space. When she makes a speech on the Senate floor, she talks like that. "You make mistakes in front of other people and laugh at yourself and move on. It's about pattern and movement and memory, and there are people of all ages in my group, as you'd know if you'd paid attention."

Mistakes in front of other people? No . . .

"Tell me about the social distance," Mom said.

"How do you ask someone to dance? How do you stay friendly and at arm's length with a partner you don't like or don't know? It's eye contact and hand contact and knowing how to make someone else feel comfortable. I've seen it work miracles for shy people."

Shy! I hate that word, and I don't think it applies, although when I speak, I have to clear my throat because it's usually been a long time since my vocal cords were used, and for no reason at all my face gets cherry red and as hot as a woodstove. . . .

"Okay," Mom said. "I agree that it might help, and right now I can't think of anything else. Mad?"

"Mom!"

"It's up to you," Mom said. "Stay here and dance, or come with me to D.C. and I'll find you a therapist." I didn't hear the sound of *maybe* in her voice, and all of a sudden I could smell hot pavement and dog-do.

"Some choice! Imprisonment and weekly torture or just weekly torture!"

Mom flicked a two-second lawyer's smile. "Exactly."

"But, *Mom!* It's not *fair!* I was being smart, I was taking care of myself, and you didn't even *know* while it was happening!"

Wrong thing to say. Mom has a real phobia about not knowing what's going on with me, and when she's phobic, she's an even better lawyer. "If invisibility was just a rational choice, Mad, and you're in perfect control, then dancing is no big deal. You're not shy, right? You don't have a problem!"

She's good! Now how could I say: But it will *kill* me to meet strangers' eyes or take their hands! I will *die* if I make a mistake in front of everyone!

I looked at Gam. She looked back, with an expression that seemed carefully blank. Was she on my side? After all, how would

Mom, way down in Washington, know if I danced? Wouldn't she have to take our word for it?

I drew a breath to speak, and their eyes sharpened on me. My heart skipped. You'd be a fool not to be afraid of these women.

"I'll stay."

Gam sank back in her chair. Mom just nodded. "What will she need for this? Special clothes?"

"Dance shoes and a skirt. I'll take care of it."

A skirt! Oh, cripes, a skirt!

"All right," Mom said. "We'd better get busy. Mother?"

"Mother what?" Gam asked, after several seconds. She wore that thousand-mile-stare again.

"Do you want to come to town with us?"

"I want more coffee," Gam said. "I want a shower. I want— aah!" The phone went off at her elbow. "I want the telephone not to ring— Hello!" A bright, careful expression formed on her face. "Certainly, I'd be glad to comment."

"Reporter," Mom said. "Let's go."

We unhitched the trailer and left it at the roadside, beside the bank of daylilies. The sun had heated up the truck cab and filled it with the scent of Mom's leftover coffee.

"I didn't leave that notebook open," I said after a minute.

"No. I opened it to see what it was."

"It was illegally obtained information. Your case should be thrown out of court."

"Nice try," Mom said. She drove in silence for a few minutes, and then she laughed. "If you ever doubt I love you, Mad, remember, I called Queen Jane at nine-thirty P.M. for you!"

A smile pushed up the corners of my mouth. I pushed them back down.

We went to Grandcourt Building Supplies, which is also the feed store, and bought shavings and fence stuff. I thought what I always think here: If things had gone differently this all might be mine. L.G., besides Long Gone, stands for Lewis Grandcourt.

But he was a minor twiglet on a large family tree, Mom always reminds me. There's a half page of Grandcourts in the local phone book. At best I'd have been a poor relation.

Gam was still on the phone when we got back. We put up the fence.

There was one already there, rusted, sagging barbed wire on wooden posts. We set up our modern plastic fence just inside it. "Dad would have loved this," Mom said as we placed the black thimble over a pencil-thin white post, tapped the post into the ground with a hammer, slid on a yellow plastic insulator, twisted the plastic wire into place. "He cut, split, and sharpened every one of those wooden posts. Then you had to make a hole in the ground with an iron bar and pound the post in with a sledgehammer. Tighten the barbed wire. Hammer in the staple. Hit your thumb. Cut yourself. Swear."

"Did you help him?"

"Oh, yes. I hated every minute of it." *Tap-tap-tap*, another white post went up. "I thought he was going to live forever."

Gamp died at fifty-six. Mom says she never realized until just lately how young that is.

She was going off to Washington, D.C.

"Ow!" I said after a minute. "This hurts, too." The fence posts are dusted with a fine white powder, minuscule shards of fiberglass that sting and prick your hands. They feel like thorns, but you can't see them.

Mom stopped tapping and looked at me. I looked back.

"Now darn it!" she said. "I was *not* going to cry!"

We hugged each other, gulped, and sniffled. "We can't give way altogether because I didn't bring any tissues," Mom said after a minute. I snickered, and so we kept our heads near the surface. But I clung hard to Mom's sturdy back, and she clung to mine.

3

MOM LEFT AT ONE, heading in the wrong direction. A mile past Gam's is a circular driveway, ideal for turning around a horse trailer. I waited on the lawn. The rumble and crunch died away. Then, taking longer than I expected, the sounds came back, and she pulled up the hill going past me. The empty trailer made a hollow rumble. Would she stop for one last hug or lean out the window and tell me something?

No. A wave, and she was gone around the corner, beyond the lilac bushes. Tiny pebbles bounced on the road and came to rest. The sound of the truck faded to nothing.

Slowly I turned and walked up the driveway, listening to my feet crunch the gravel. Gam's bedroom shades were drawn; she was napping. A breeze made the columbines nod, and the lawn rippled like a pony's mane.

Cloud nickered when she saw me. "Hi, girlfriend," I said. "Let's get you outside."

Cloud's life had been entirely artificial: stalls, indoor arenas, grassless paddocks. Would she be afraid?

No. She took five bouncy steps, tail high and sweeping. She looked at the apple trees, the fence, the old claw-foot bathtub full of water. Then with a big sigh she dropped her head to eat.

It was exactly what I'd wanted to see: my pretty white horse, my indoor horse, knee-deep in grass. As so often when you get exactly what you want, I felt a wormhole of unease in my chest. I hadn't painted myself into this scene. What would *I* be doing while my horse grazed?

Hanging out with Gam, that's what. I guess even before Leslie's e-mail I'd been expecting to get something important from Gam this summer. Not that Mom isn't tough and brave, but what she does is more private. It's a contest, with a judge or jury to decide who wins or loses. Gam was out in public with a lot of people hating her guts, and she never let that stop her. If I could get what she has, the courage to sail into a fight instead of shrinking back, high school would be all right. I could get us through.

I just wanted to get started. That was the only reason I felt uneasy.

Inside, a red light blinked on the answering machine: nine messages. As I passed, the number broke up, the red flashes rotated, and a ten appeared. It seemed like a lot of calls, even for the Powerful Chair.

I got a screwdriver from Gamp's toolbox and tiptoed past her closed door, upstairs to my room.

This was Mom's room when she was a girl and again after L.G. left. She brought me here from the hospital, and we shared the room for five years while she worked her way through law school. It's small, made dark by the patterned blue wallpaper, crowded by the two beds. But I would never change it. It puts its arms around me with a healing peace whenever I walk in.

There was only one thing I wanted different, and that was easy. The mirror attached to the bureau by screws. It came off to reveal an even darker patch of wallpaper and a lot of cobwebs. I put it in the closet. Then I risked a glance.

A mirror tilted backward in dim closet light would make most people look tall and elegant and mysterious. Not a Parker. We are sultry as teddy bears, rangy as Shetland ponies.

This body is fine for an old lady. Mom, the killer barracuda lawyer, finds it good camouflage. But who wants to go out with a girl who's built like a milk crate? Who's freckled and snub-nosed and at best occasionally cute? Not that there's anyone I want to go out with, but I'd like to be in the position of turning down applicants!

"Good-bye," I said to my reflection, and started to turn away. The boxes in the closet caught my eye.

They were full of things Mom had left behind, and they held no secrets from me. I've read her school papers and her love poems. I know who her old boyfriends were, what brand of cigarette she used during her two weeks as a smoker—everything. I knew where the picture and the notes were, and it took just a minute to dig them out.

L.G. was (is?) left-handed. His handwriting had a steep forward slant, as if running to keep from tipping over. He wrote to Mom, "I'm picking up pizza—don't cook. Hope you're feeling better than you did this morning." He wrote, "I'm sorry I didn't say the right thing last night. Of course I'm happy." He wrote, "I need to be alone for a while to think things through. Don't worry."

That was the last note. He never came back. After a month his mother sent for his clothes but wouldn't say where he'd gone. Mom got a divorce a few weeks before I was born, so I don't even carry his name.

In his picture he is thin and rumpled. A mane of frizzy red-blond hair stands out around his head. The picture was taken while he was still in high school. Maybe he was bald now. Maybe that hippie mane was cut short, and he wore a suit and tie all day.

I didn't want to know, really. I didn't want him back.

I did, though. I wanted him to come home someday and see me, brave and beautiful, a perfect rider, and I wanted his heart to break with pride and regret. I wanted him to kick himself for the rest of his life that he had missed seeing me grow up. But he couldn't come back yet. He had to wait till I got better at things.

I also wanted to understand my inheritance from him. I didn't get the name or the long legs. I got psoriasis. I got cowardice and a talent for secrecy. When Mom asked, "What are you turning into?" it was L.G.'s soft, vague smile I saw.

I wedged his picture into the mirror frame and closed the door.

The rest of moving in was simpler. Clothes in the bureau-drawers; I never wear anything you'd hang on a hanger. Books on the shelf. Pictures on the bureau: Cloud, Leslie on Brando, Mom with our old dog that died. On the pockmarked bulletin board I pinned a photo of Jane riding in her long-tailed coat and top hat. The white-gloved fingers of her right hand combed through a set of double reins and curled around a whip handle. She slanted a severe glance along the wall, seeming to deplore the dusty, curling magazine picture of Larry Mahan hanging beside her.

Larry Mahan was a rodeo champion. Mom had a crush on him in third grade, and his picture has hung there ever since. By now he must be old enough to be my grandfather, but in this picture he is forever cute, forever young. I like Larry Mahan. I left him right where he was.

After a while I heard movement downstairs and went to find Gam at the stove, making macaroni and cheese out of a box.

"Yes, I know," she said.

"I didn't say—"

"But everything in the refrigerator is growing fur, and we'll get refreshments at the dance. Look at this! Do we even want to speculate how they get it this color?"

She seemed alarmingly perky. I'd been assuming she'd be too tired to go to the dance, but clearly that wasn't the case. I set the table and got out glasses.

"Better stick to soda," Gam said.

I opened the refrigerator. "There's milk." But when I picked it up, something thunked inside the carton. I looked at the date. "*Gam!* You've had this since *February!*"

She just nodded. During the session Gam shares an apartment with several colleagues. The legislature meets Tuesday through Friday, so in theory she's home three days a week. In truth those days are spent on the phone or back at the Statehouse working. The refrigerator is left to its own devices.

We sat down to our orange supper. "So," I said, with a glance at the clock, "will we pick up the Cat tonight?"

"No time. Dance starts at eight. I have to get dressed and stop at the store to pick up my veggie platter and some milk you can actually pour."

"I don't own a skirt," I said. "Just so you know."

"That's all right, you won't be dancing. Stay in your jeans and no one will ask you. I want you to make a good first impression on Morag."

"If not dancing is what it takes, I'll make a good first impression! I'll make a good seven*teenth* impression!"

"Oh, I think not," Gam said. She seemed both cheerful and distant; I had the feeling she was occupied, just below the surface, with other things.

After supper she said, "Better go put your horse in while I change."

"Put her in?"

"She can't stay on that rich grass too long at first," Gam said. "She'll colic or founder."

"Oh." I couldn't believe I hadn't thought of that. Jane hadn't mentioned it either. "Thanks. I forgot."

"Well, I still remember a thing or two about the real world!" Gam put the dishes in the sink and glanced at the clock. "Better hurry."

I walked out with a lead rope. Cloud walked in the opposite direction.

"Hey!" I yelled. "Whoa!"

Cloud, the horse some people call sickeningly well behaved, walked faster. I made a move to head her off. She accelerated: beautiful medium trot. In a dressage test I'd have given her high marks.

"You can't stay out! You'll get *sick*!" Running after her now. Stupid. I couldn't possibly catch her, and she knew it.

I stopped. This was the horse I rode yesterday, medium canter between K and H, buttery soft as a doeskin glove; the horse that every day took exactly five steps out of her stall, swung her quarters around, and stood waiting at the crossties, a sound so measured and regular I could hear it in my dreams: defying me. The pasture was broad; the grass waved; it could take all night to catch her—

All night!

I started walking again, Cloud started walking, and that was how Gam found us ten minutes later, when she came out in her long white dress.

"I can't catch her!" I called. "You'd better go without me."

Gam didn't answer for a moment. Then she shouted, "Did you try grain?"

Rats! "No."

Gam didn't say anything more, just stood in the driveway while I went for a dipper of grain. Cloud reached for it, and I thought of spooking her. But Gam would see, and besides, I'd need to catch this horse tomorrow. I let her put her nose in the dipper and snapped the rope onto her halter.

As I led her through the gate, Gam said, "Nice try, Mad!"

4

I LIKE BARRETT. The width of its Main Street and the shape of its buildings seem right for a town. The city where we live now seems too open to the sky. The streets are too wide, the buildings too low, and the sunlight comes in wrong—harshly, always finding the ugly side of things. Even the lake, at the bottom of the rolling streets, seems wrong to me. Only sometimes, when it's very blue and the triangles of sail glide across it, do I like the lake, and even then it's farther away than it appears.

In Barrett, though, some things are too close. Like the three ladies who came up to me—one in the library, two in the grocery store—and each separately said, "My God, it takes me back twenty years! You're Maddy Parker, aren't you? You look *just* like your mother!"

"Are you sure I wasn't *cloned?*" I muttered to Gam as we followed our squeaking grocery cart away from lady number three.

"No, you were arrived at by natural methods!" Gam's upper lip came to a point, as it does when she's saying something sarcastic. The lip was about all I could see of her face. The rest was hidden behind enormous round sunglasses that gave her all the anonymity they ever gave Jackie Onassis.

We veered around the end of the aisle, and someone said, "Hi, Liz!"

"It's not working!" I whispered. "They can tell who you are!"

"They can also tell that I don't want to talk." Gam reached for a box of cereal, a kind we both detest.

"You can't even *see!*" I put the sweet crunchies back on the shelf and took down a box of plain cornflakes. "Come on, Gam! Lose the shades!"

"My, my," she said sweetly. "This takes me back twenty years! *Just* the way your mother used to criticize me!"

The dance was at the elementary school. We went through a side door into a kitchen full of women in dresses, fussing with covered dishes. "My grandaughter, Madeline Parker," Gam said at large. "She'll be dancing with us this summer. I won't introduce you individually, Mad, and then they can't expect you to remember their names." She set her vegetable platter on the table and breezed through the inner door to the gym, sweeping me in her wake.

The gym had been decorated with posters and tartan hangings, but school-gymness swallowed Scottishness. The lights in a school gym vibrate orange. The windows are always high and always closed, and the doors look small and distant. If you broke for one, it would be like a dream where you can't scream and you can't run. The lady with the mustache will catch you, and you'll have to play basketball forever.

This gym was nearly empty. At one end of the room a woman in white was setting up a CD player, and across from us someone bent to lace a dance slipper. That skirt's riding pretty high! I remember thinking, and I'd shave my thighs if they were that hairy—

Then the person straightened and turned, and was a guy. A man? A boy—slim, broad-shouldered, blue-eyed, and blond. He wore a white shirt with ruffles down the front and a skirt—

No, a kilt. They're called kilts. It was short, just above knee length, pleated in back, flat in front, and where a gentleman might want a fig leaf hung a flat leather pouch with tassels. Below that he wore—there would be another term than *knee socks* to describe them. They looked hand knit, with thick braids of cable, and sticking out the top of one was a bone knife handle.

I think I didn't gape at him. I think I saw this all in one discreet glance because within seconds Gam had led me to the woman at the CD player.

"Morag, I'd like you to meet my grandaughter, Madeline, who's spending the summer with me. Madeline, this is Morag McAe, our dance instructor."

Pale blue, glittering eyes stared at me, unblinking. I was already rattled and looked down, but her gaze bored into the top of my head and seemed to lift my eyes up to meet hers. Yike! I thought. But she was only a plain, thin-lipped woman with a smooth cap of gray hair.

"Hello, Madeline. Will you be comin' dancin' then?"

My voice stuck for a second and then came out too forcefully. "Yes!"

"D'you have any experience?"

"N-no!" We learned a Norwegian folk dance in third grade, I almost told her. Somehow I stopped myself.

"Good, you'll have nothing to unlearn." She turned back to her CD player, and I followed Gam over to the chairs along the wall, mouthing to myself, Unlairn. Unlairn.

Gam sat down to put on her slippers. "Gillies. They're called gillies," she said. I sank down beside her, watching as the beautiful young man walked over to Morag. Amazing how great a guy can look in a skirt! The kilt hugged his hips and swung free below. The knife-sharp pleats swayed to his step. He spoke to Morag, too quietly for me to hear, and she said, "Aye, Neil, y'might do that." He crossed the floor again and went down the hall behind us. Neil. His name was Neil.

People were coming in steadily: older men and women, young people who might be in high school or might be in college. Neil must be in college—definitely not high school.

So many people, and I didn't know any of them. I liked that. I could enjoy them as scenery: the natural swagger of the kilts, the colorful formality. Some men wore black jackets and black vests with glittering buttons. Women and girls wore laces, sequins, limp white cotton, stiff ruby taffeta. I saw plunging necklines and high ruffles and every stage in between.

Neil again: He brought a wooden school desk to Morag. He helped a red-haired girl spread a tablecloth on a long school table. People were changing their shoes, stretching their calf muscles, standing together in stiff little knots. Some gathered near Gam, and I noticed how her voice began to warm and relax—

"Tree huggers!" I heard a man nearby say in one of those

unpleasant voices that are meant to be overheard. Gam flushed and turned her head as a burst of music sounded.

"Take partners, please," Morag said, "for the Gay Gordons!"

What does that mean? I was wondering when Gam took my hands and pulled me to my feet.

"But—you *said*—"

"Everyone does the Gay Gordons. You don't need to know how." She drew me into the line of people that circled the room, two by two, facing counterclockwise.

"No!" I pulled toward the chairs. Gam's hands tightened, and the music started.

Gam lifted my right hand up by my right shoulder, so I was tucked under her arm. She held my left hand waist-high, and marched me forward four steps: "One, two, three, four" in my ear. Then she switched me to march backward, still in the same direction. "One, two, three, four." Then forward, going back the way we'd come—"One, two, three, four"—and switch, backward: "One, two, three, four."

Then she let go of my left hand and twirled me by my right, still held high, while she danced in place—"one, two, three, four"— and now she had me in her arms. "And polka, one, two, three, four." My feet stumbled, my knees hit hers, and still she whisked me around, circling, till we came to rest facing counterclockwise, and she got me in the over-the-shoulder grip again. "March—one, two, three, four."

It went on and on and on. Gam hardly met my eyes. She was looking past me, a frown cutting sharp lines between her brows. When she did notice me, she made a face, not quite smiling, not quite apologetic. "You're doing fine, Mad."

A lump formed in my throat. She had to know how awful this was. She's going to make me do it! I thought. She's really going to make me!

At last the music stopped. Gam swung me to face her and curt-sied, panting slightly. "There! Your first dance! Not that bad, huh?"

I just looked at her. I couldn't push a single word past the lump in my throat, and what could I say? What could I possibly say?

We made for the chairs. The room was louder now, with a light, relieved, laughing sound in the air.

After a moment Morag's powerful voice cut through. "Welcome to the spring social of the Barrett Scottish Country Dance Group. Glad you could all come. The first dance on the program tonight is The Machine Without Horses—"

A white-haired man in a kilt came up to Gam and held out his hand. "Would you like to do this one?"

"Yes, thank you." Gam put her hand in his, and he led her toward the top of the room. She glanced over her shoulder at me. "Mad, just say no."

I had a better idea. Thirty seconds later I was out the door, heading down the school driveway and up the long hill out of town.

I walked fast. My legs scissored the distance, up the ribbon of blacktop.

Furious! I thought. I'm *furious*! How could Gam do that to me? She must have been known how awful it was! How *could* she?

Gradually I noticed where I was, hot, out of breath, and high above the village. There were just a few houses scattered beside the road. I passed two little kids in a yard. They had tiny white objects in their hands, and as I went by, they shook the things at me and squinched up their faces. "Eeny meeny meeny!"

"Eeny meeny meeny!"

"You both look stupid!" I said, but I think they didn't hear me. My voice came thick and low, and their faces didn't change. I blundered on up the hill, big and dull and mean.

Gordie and I used to do things like that. He was my kindergarten best friend. We kidnapped people and tied them up with those thin cotton strings that stitch together grain bags. We jumped out at people and roared like lions. One day it was Mom we ambushed. She'd come to say she'd gotten her first law job, and we had to move.

My heart swelled against my chest wall. I *missed* Gordie! I missed Leslie. I missed the barn, where no matter what they thought even the Clubbers let me alone, because Jane's disapproval was the End of the World. I wanted my own stall, and the tack trunk in front, and nice sarcastic Nesta and George, the accountant, even the hot apartment. Even the sidewalks.

Mom was in the air now, heading toward Washington.

The road climbed more steeply. No houses for a while, and then one with six junk cars in the yard. The crest of the hill was still far above me, and my legs felt heavy.

A car climbed the hill behind me. That would be Gam. She'd stop beside me, and her eyes would shoot flame—

The car whooshed past and disappeared over the crest of the hill.

I stopped. Where was I going? I felt small and slow. "Like an ant," I said. "I feel like an ant." The dark woods rose on either side, and the dark road rose in front of me. My legs felt heavy.

Without deciding anything, I turned back. Soon I could see the gym door standing open. Light and music came out thin and small, like one of those fairy dances seen through a crack in the side of a hill, which lure the unwary to their doom.

5

WHEN A NIGHT TRAVELER sees a light shining from a hillside, and peeks, and is lost, the fatal error is usually food. Fairy food makes the traveler forget the true world for fifty, a hundred, a thousand years.

But I'd walked four miles, I found out later, and the moment I reached the door the music stopped and Morag said, "We'll have refreshments now." A thirsty crowd thronged the punch bowl. Ordinarily I'd have kept my distance, but I was thirsty, too. A cup of punch, a deviled egg, two cheese straws—from that moment perhaps there was really no choice.

The dancers looked warm. The men's shirts were soaked with sweat, and all the black jackets with their shiny buttons hung on the backs of chairs. I drifted, eating, and no one spoke to me. A girl in blue jeans, I was clearly not one of them.

Some of the older people had Scottish accents. Listening, I realized how badly people mangle Scottish when they imitate it. I will never do that, I thought, while my tongue silently tried out the shape of the vowels.

"Did y'go back last year?"

"Aye, in June"—Jun, I mouthed. Jün? The *u* was soft and short—"rained every bloody day!"

The posters on the gym walls, put out by the Scottish Tourist Board, showed castles, lochs, highlands, under brilliant blue skies. Just like our tourist posters! There were lots of pictures of thistles— the national flower, I guess.

I found Gam drinking coffee and talking with Morag. "What do you think so far?" she asked.

"Aye," said Morag, "are y'enjoyin' it then?" She seemed looser, happier, but how sharp those cold blue eyes seemed. I didn't dare lie.

"I went for a walk."

"Watch during the second half," Morag said. Her eyes were unwavering. Didn't she ever *blink*? "If you get some idea of what's going on, it'll make my job easier."

"Yes." I looked down into my cup and said, "I . . . think I'll get some more punch."

Morag announced the end of intermission and a dance called Haddington Assembly. Feeling underwaterish and faraway, I watched the lines form, men facing women the length of the gym. Morag made a short, incomprehensible speech, apparently telling them how to do the dance. "Finishing with mirror reels," she said.

The dancers exchanged uncertain looks. Some drew pictures in the air with their fingers.

Morag's voice amplified over the swelling murmur. "Twos dance up and out, threes dance up and in, ones dance straight down and cast up through third couple's position. D'you want to walk it?"

Some people nodded vigorously, but a loud chorus of noes at the top of the room won out. Morag pushed a button on the CD player.

A chord sounded, everyone bowed or curtsied, and they were off. Some couples skimmed down between the lines, back up and around, dancing in place for a moment, looping out again. I found Neil and the red-haired girl. They seemed to float on the music.

Then everyone was moving at once, curving toward each other close enough to brush shoulders, and then away, and back, couples weaving in and out. It was perfect, like dancing with yourself in the mirror, and it seemed to repeat and repeat as the music went on: a single couple doing most of the dancing, and then the mirror reel again.

Once the sound of voices made me look down the room. There the mirror was broken. Dancers were milling around, looking bewildered, and a short, stout man in a kilt was shouting, "This way! Up!" Some people had come to a complete standstill.

My stomach lurched. I could see myself down there!

Someone squeaked down onto the folding chair beside me. Out the corner of my eye I saw a kilt, young knees, young hands with bitten nails . . .

"You don't remember me, do you?"

I was startled enough to look straight at him: big, around my age, with dark, wavy hair and a fabulous nose. It was a man's nose, large and sort of undulating; it made me think of George Washington. His eyes were brown and smiling. I did know those eyes. Didn't I?

"It's Gordie," he said. "Hi."

"Gordie? But—you don't have a nose like that!"

He put his hand up to his face and took it away again quickly. Patches of red colored his cheeks. "C'mon, Mad, I was five years old! It grew, all right?"

"But—but I was just thinking about you!" I couldn't stop staring at the nose. When I knew him, it was a cute little button.

"You look just the same," he said.

The heat came up in my face. It's what you've always dreamed of, isn't it? Meet an old flame, and he tells you you still look five years old!

"Well, you *do*," he said after a minute. Something in the way he insisted made me look at him again, and now I could see him in the sandbox with the big yellow dump truck, saying, "No, the road goes *this* way!" Were we really the same people? I looked five, he sounded it, but we couldn't really *be* the same, could we? In those days we liked to kidnap people. Now—

"Do you still like horses?" he asked.

"Yes. Do you still like trucks?"

He looked down at his bare knees and shook his head. "Not that much."

"Oh." Now I should ask another question. I knew that was how you kept a conversation going. But ask what? Hey, remember those graham crackers? And taking naps on our mats?

"You're staying for the whole summer?" he asked.

"Yes."

"Are you coming to dance classes?"

Well, that was the question, wasn't it? I turned to look at him, in his dark kilt, his shirt with ruffles at the throat. "Are you Scottish?"

"With a name like Gordon McIver, what else would I be?"

I'd never known his last name. He was just Gordie when we were five. The Gordon McIver I knew about was a state senator, an R, Gam's toughest opponent. "Are you related—"

The flush on his cheekbones deepened. "Senator McIver is my grandfather."

I glanced up the hall. Gam was at one of those mysterious standstills and looking across the room at me. Was I supposed to be talking with Gordie McIver? Was he supposed to be talking with me?

"Do you know everybody here?" I asked. "Who's the girl with red hair?" It was beautiful hair, flowing past her shoulders in a crumpled stream. It made Neil easy to spot, no matter how thick the crowd.

"That's Sumner," he said. "Sumner Grandcourt." He made his voice flat and neutral. He liked Sumner, liked her the way Romeo liked Juliet.

A Grandcourt. She would be! Graceful and beautiful, like so many of them. It was typical of Gam that her genes dominated even the Grandcourts'.

"Who's she dancing with?"

Gordie gave me a disgusted look that took me straight back to the sandbox. "That's Neil Bishop. *All* the girls like him—*and* he's in college!" Like I needed that to make him off-limits! "So's Sumner," he added after a moment.

Heat flooded my face. The music stopped with a final chord. The dancers bowed and curtsied, and Gam came over. "Hello, Gordie. I'm glad you two have met."

"We already knew each other," Gordie said. "We were best friends in kindergarten."

"You were?" Gam looked from him to me. "I didn't remember that."

A woman in a pale blue dress bustled up to us. "Did you make it through that last dance? We fell apart completely! You, Gordie, why did you sit out? Chicken!"

She seemed like a person who didn't notice other people's body language—perfect. I stepped back, and back again, and vanished into the hall.

The light was dim here. There were people, but not very many. I took a deep breath, throwing back my shoulders.

"Hi," someone said beside me. I turned and looked into Neil Bishop's sparkling blue eyes.

He smiled. "You must be—"

I ducked my head and hurried past him; light shining through a low grate told me I'd reached the bathroom door. I pushed it open.

It was the kilts that confused me, just for a second. Skirts would normally mean Women's Room, but the face looking over the shoulder wore a beard and seemed very startled.

A warm hand caught my upper arm. "Wrong door," said a deep, amused voice, and I was in the hall again, staring in horror at Neil's ruffled shirtfront. "Girls' Room is down that way—no." The hand caught me again and gave me a little push in the right direction.

My whole body broke out in sweat. I plunged through the door and into a stall, sank onto the teeny grade school–size commode, and pressed my hands to my face. "Oh, my God! Oh, my God!" The separate moments of horror ran through my mind like slow-motion replays: I don't answer him in the hall; I push open the men's room door; the bearded face; the hand . . . "Oh, my God!"

Women's voices approached. The door opened as someone said, ". . . work pretty well."

"You don't find them too thick?" The Powerful Chair. Too late to pull my feet up; I stayed still, hoping she'd think I was here for the usual reasons.

"No, they squash down, but they really cushion the impact." The silken, rustling sounds of large ladies in nylons. They took stalls on either side of me. The conversation about shock-absorbing foot pads continued. Hand washing, hairbrushing, mirror gazing, departure. The door sighed shut and then opened again, and Gam said softly, "Mad?"

I thought of not answering. She went into the stall beside me. I heard the door latch click and the toilet lid close, and she sat down. "Yeah," I said.

"Hiding out?"

"Mmm."

She said after a moment, "I like the Statehouse ladies' room better. For a hideout."

Don't tell me this! "When? When do you ever hide out in the ladies' room?"

She gave an odd laugh. "My colleagues think I have an intestinal disorder!"

"When?"

"When Rachel held that little meeting, for one! You heard about that?"

The whole state had heard about it. The governor, Rachel Hessian, is a "moderate D." Moderate supposedly means you look at both sides of a question. What it means for Rachel Hessian, according to the Powerful Chair, is you never take a controversial stand, and you play both ends against the middle. Rachel Hessian's goal— says the Powerful Chair—is to become a U.S. senator just like the one we have now, a hermaphrodite, as the Powerful Chair likes to call him, half D and half R.

When Gam's committee was deadlocked on the tax cut, Governor Hessian called them into her office. Only two people weren't invited: Gam and her closest ally. If Gam hadn't found out in time, Rachel Hessian would have made a deal between the Rs and the moderate Ds. She'd have been the heroine of the year.

But Gam did find out, and then the press did, and then everyone did. Rachel Hessian's star was tarnished just a little, and a week later a better deal was made, by the Powerful Chair of the Finance Committee.

"After that meeting," Gam said, "we had a fight in her office. She said, 'Who do you think you are, Parker? Just *who* do you think you are?' 'I think I'm an influential member of your party, Rachel,' I said, 'and I think you just made a big mistake.' Then I recessed my committee for fifteen minutes and hid in the ladies' room."

"Did you cry?"

She didn't exactly answer. "I flushed the toilet whenever somebody came in." Her slippered feet kicked restlessly. "Every time I moved a piece of paper the rest of the day I could see it shake. But you know what? Nobody else could!"

She went quiet. I sat on my side of the yellow wall, trying to imagine her crying, flushing for cover. Papers shaking in her hand. I really, really didn't want to know that—

"Mad?"

"Mmm?"

"Why are you in here?"

She's good! She'd lulled and distracted me until now it seemed impossible not to tell. "I walked in on somebody peeing. In the men's room."

"Oh, poor Maddie! But you know what? Men don't seem to care about that. You do, I do, but they don't, and let's just be thankful."

"Neil Bishop was right behind me!" My face went hot again.

"My darling girl," Gam said.

She fell silent. The concrete walls filtered the music. Only the bass came through, thumping and insistent. Washington, D.C., wouldn't be *all* pavement and dog poop, I thought. I could go to museums, libraries. I could stand it.

Gam sighed. "I don't want to go back out either."

"Why not?"

She gave a sad-sounding laugh. "I had an important achievement, too! I got a bill passed to ban clear-cut logging in this state. And I got Rachel to agree to sign it." She stood up in her little yellow stall. "Grandcourt Brothers were going to sell three thousand acres here to an outside company. The Grandcourts don't clear-cut, but the new guys would have. Now the deal's off."

"And it's your fault?"

Gam said, "I didn't do it alone, but it wouldn't have happened without me. The Grandcourts know that, and tomorrow everybody in the state finds out."

"Let's just go home."

"Morag wouldn't like that. C'mon, Mad, better now than later."

She opened her stall door. I sat still. "I—do I have to? Dance, I mean?"

"Not tonight!"

"But . . . ever?"

"Yes. That's what you agreed to."

"But . . . she wouldn't make me go to D.C., would she? Really?"

"I never call your mother's bluff, Mad. I don't want to find out which of us is tougher."

She sounded exhausted all of a sudden. My heart sank. This wasn't how it was supposed to be. She was supposed to be giving me courage, not the other way around.

But I couldn't say no. I opened the stall door. "Thank you," Gam said.

I couldn't even pick out the man I'd walked in on, and Neil Bishop never glanced at me. So that worked out.

I watched the patterns formed by the dancers: spinning stars and figure eights, squares and ladders, lazy S curves. Sometimes people stood still for a while and then abruptly swung into motion. How did they know when to start and when to stop? It must be in the music, but all I could hear was the wild, swift beat and the yelping fiddles.

I liked the crisp flick of the kilts. I liked the skipping, skimming step. I liked watching Neil, and I liked how even old women like Gam became light and frisky. I liked the little yell that Morag gave, low and thin and almost private, with a yelp on the end like the fiddles: "ee-EE-*YEOUGH!*" I liked watching Neil.

But every few minutes my stomach sank, and I realized, Monday night *I'll* have to do this!

6

SUNDAY MORNING I had an e-mail from Leslie.

```
From: lesismor@v.net
To: madwoman@v.net
Subject: your stall

Guess who jane gave me for a neighbor??!!
aleika! aleika! she actually *moved aleika*
out of Club Row and put a grown-up over
there. I said *jane!* She said she didn't
want her barn turning into a bunch of
exclusive suburbs and this was a good
chance to mix things up. i said but when
Mad comes back?? and she said *we'll
see*!!!!
```

No time to answer; Gam wanted to go out that minute for the papers.

We sat in the parking lot, with rain sheeting across the windshield. I read the comics, and Gam read the interviews she'd given on Saturday. One rated a snort, one a serious, approving nod, and at the third her lip became very pointed.

There were pictures of clear-cuts in all the papers: bare ground, stumps, and tangled tops, large machines feasting on whole trees. Reporters explained that clear-cut logging meant cutting every tree on a piece of land, whether you could use it or not. It was faster and more efficient than traditional methods. It caused erosion. It choked streams with mud. It looked like war.

The answering machine voices sounded like war. Gam had voted to fund a highway bypass she'd fought for years, a pet project of Governor Hessian's. Even people who loved the clear-cut bill were mad at her. All afternoon, while I turned Cloud out in the rain, and got her in again, and made oatmeal cookies, Gam explained.

"Count the votes. She was going to get the bypass anyway. I saw a chance to get something in exchange."

"It was a horse trade. You can't get something for nothing."

"I agree, but sometimes you just have to bite the bullet."

But did she really? Some people on the answering machine sounded shocked. "I never thought I'd see Liz Parker's name on a vote like that! It just shows you can't ever trust a politician, no matter how good they seem!" Gam listened to this lady's voice with pencil poised to take the phone number. Her head was down, and I couldn't see her face.

It was late afternoon before Mom finally got through. The apartment was little and white, she said. It was hot out.

I was glad to hear her voice, but I couldn't think what to say either. Last night's dance was nothing I ever wanted to relive. We said good-bye, the phone rang for Gam, and I put on the Spanish Riding School video.

It belongs to the Barrett library, but it's really mine. I was in fifth grade when I first watched it, at the kicking-ponies-over-jumps stage, but the moment I saw the dancing white stallions I wanted to join that dance, more than anything in the world.

Even in fifth grade I couldn't help noticing that all the riders are men, and it's useless to think that will ever change. They have been doing things exactly that way for hundreds of years, and that's sort of the point. But they do give lessons to outsiders, the video shows a woman getting one, and someday . . .

Meanwhile I fell in love with Cloud, the white dressage horse, and began learning the modern art, which is not a dance of horses together, but competition, riders one at a time putting horses through an identical routine, being judged and ranked. If you looked at it from very far away—like another planet—maybe you'd see something that looks like a dance. But from down here winning is what matters.

At the Spanish Riding School beauty wins. Through a lot of ugly history, through Hitler and World War II even, they kept making beauty and kindness and peace.

Today I replayed the quadrille. The horses approach, turn away, pass and repass, reflecting one another as if in a mirror. Last night in the school gym, beneath the Scottish tourist posters, I'd seen human dancers do things like that.

The horses were more beautiful. The camera panned the rows of white legs sidestepping across the school, perfectly at ease, in perfect unison. There were no mistakes, ever.

There's one dark horse in every performance. On the tape he seems like a dark spot on the mirror. Why does the riding school do that? I always wonder. If I were sitting there in real life, free to move my eyes, I'd always watch the dark horse. He'd seem more beautiful, yet not perfect like the others.

They say the Navajo weavers take care to make one mistake in each cloth, to avoid seeming arrogant and attracting the gods' attention. I don't get that. What's wrong with perfection?

At the end of the afternoon Gam apologized. "This isn't how it's going to be. All this will die down in a few days, and we'll have our summer. Now, are you hungry? Faith said she'd feed us when we pick up the Cat."

I had never lived with the Cat. He moved in after Mom and I moved out. Gam still kept up the fiction that she was looking for a home for him. Meanwhile he received royal care and spent the session with Faith Hamborough.

Faith lived in India as a child, and her house is full of Indian things, from the smell of curry when we walked into the kitchen to the elephants, all sizes and all kinds of wood and metal, marching across the top of her bookcase. She's Gam's dearest friend; the elephants are among the earliest things I can remember.

The Cat crouched on a kitchen chair, turning his large tiger-and-white back to us. Gam bent and made coaxing noises. The Cat gave her a long, yellow, disillusioned stare and stalked off.

"He's taken that attitude since about May first," Faith said. "Like reporters, he doesn't like a long session!"

When Faith smiles, she shows a lot of teeth. Her own, I think; they stick out, and they're ivory-colored, not even and white like dentures. She has a large face with skin that seems to drape in soft crinkles. She's tall and bony and—

Oh! I thought. She's a lot older than Gam!

I think of old people as being all the same age, but tonight Faith seemed elderly and fragile. Why was *she* making *us* supper? I watched her walk to the stove; her feet seemed to grope for the floor. "Can I help?"

"No, Mad, I just need to give this a stir. It's good to see you! What will you do this summer?"

"She's going to come dancing with me," Gam said.

"Oh, isn't that nice! I used to love to dance! When Morag started the Scottish lessons, I tried, but I can't anymore. I could feel every bone in my feet, as clear as an X ray."

"I wish we could trade feet," I said. "Then you could dance and I wouldn't have to!"

"Don't you like it?"

"She doesn't know yet," Gam said.

"Oh, it's the best thing, Mad!" Faith half turned, her face glowing. Something red-brown and spicy-looking drizzled from her spoon to the stovetop. "Dancing is like . . . *being* the music. There's almost nothing better."

"What I'm mostly going to do is ride," I said. "I've never gotten to ride on dirt roads or in the woods, and neither has Cloud."

Faith said, "I wonder if she'll be frightened."

"She's been to lots of horse shows, before I owned her. She's seen a lot of stuff. But she never gets to just go straight and get somewhere. It's always circles. Lots and lots of circles."

"And you want to tear off cross-country for a change! Good for you!" Faith stirred and bent to sniff the aromatic steam. "This is almost ready. Would you mind setting the dining room table, Mad?"

I know where things are in Faith's house nearly as well as in Gam's. I got out plates, folded napkins in perfect triangles, opened the velvet-lined silverware box with its special, nose-tickling smell—

"After you play hardball, you hurt." Faith's almost breaking shell of a voice, out in the kitchen. They'd been speaking right along, but I hadn't paid attention. "At least you and I do. You think you should have done better—"

"Or not at all!" Gam said.

"How did you bring it off?"

"The votes were there for the bypass, but I got Corey and Sue and McIver not to say which way they'd vote, and when she got worried enough, I offered her a deal: We'd support the bypass if she'd support the clear-cut bill."

"So the bypass is going to happen?"

"It was going to happen no matter what way I voted. But most people think it's better to go down in flames than make a horse trade."

"They live in perfect ignorance of their own political system," Faith said. "You can't take judgments of that kind seriously. I realized that a long time ago."

How does Faith know this stuff? I wondered. Something stirred at the back of my brain. I shut the silverware box and looked up, and right in front of me, on the inlaid wood table, was a photograph of Faith, a younger-old Faith, sitting at a familiar curved desk in the Senate chamber.

Oh, yes. Faith was a senator, a long time ago.

Out in the kitchen Gam was saying, ". . . one of the rare times when I know we're right. But maybe I did it wrong."

"You did it the way you could."

"But sometimes that contaminates things. Maybe I should have waited, gotten a consensus—"

"You got a majority," Faith said. "People from both parties. In my day we called that a consensus—or as good as!"

"Yes. Well, it's too late," Gam said. "Mad, that table ready?" She raised her voice, as if I couldn't hear them perfectly well.

"All set," I said, and they came in with the fragrant curry and the pitcher of cider.

*   *   *

"I'd forgotten Faith was a senator," I said on the way home.

"Almost everyone has. That's what happens. One day you're a Very Important Person, and the next you're nobody. Look! A star! You'll have a nice day for riding tomorrow."

Before bed I finally got a chance to e-mail Leslie.

```
To: lesismor@v.net
From: madwoman@v.net
Subject: my stall

what does jane mean, we'll see?????
I have to dance! All summer, every Monday
night, with a Scotswoman named Morag
teaching—it's the price for not keeping
the Invisibility Project perfectly
invisible.
I'll be dancing with guys in skirts. Short
pleated skirts. And knee-sox. With knives
in them.
I met Gordie, my kindergarten best friend,
at the dance. He has the most outstanding
nose, and he is nice! See? Even when I
was 5 years old, I picked a good person to
be friends with!
Morag makes Jane seem like Tinker Bell.
So, Aleika. What's she like-a?
```

7

AT HOME I ride early. Often it's still dark when I lead Cloud into the Indoor Arena. It's quiet. Cars outside, horses rattling their buckets. I ride circles and serpentines, spirals and figure eights, listening to Cloud's muffled footfalls, trying to keep them steady through each turn and shape. In the mirrors I ride toward myself, alongside, away, dancing a quadrille with my own reflection. I can pretend: The walls are white and gilt, not brown; music is playing; and my reflection and I have a dozen other counterparts filing behind us, crisscrossing in front.

By the time Mom gets back from the gym, hair damp and shampoo-smelling on her shoulders, I'm untacking Cloud in the aisle, hosing her down and blanketing her, doling out the sugar cubes. Then I shower and climb into my dark disguise, ready for another invisible day.

So it was early when I started on my first ride here. I meant to sleep late, but I hadn't learned how yet, and it was only seven-fifteen when we headed down the driveway.

The sky was brilliant blue, and wind rippled the puddles. The world seemed wide around us: no walls, no mirrors, just fields and woods and dirt roads.

Mom used to ride down the middle of this road. No cars ever came. This morning a car passed every five minutes. Cloud wasn't afraid; Catamount Stables is next to a busy highway, with trucks passing all day long. Not even the school bus made her do more than prick her ears.

Was Gordie on that bus? Where did he live? I couldn't remember. The bus disappeared around a bend in the road. A little boy made faces out the back window. I smiled back. I was free. *He* had two more weeks of school.

The road came to a Y; I turned uphill on Vesper Road, and the cars stopped coming. Ten feet above me, atop a steep bank, the trunks of maple trees rose out of the leaf litter. A barbed-wire fence strung the trees together, and there was a field beyond. Below me the land dropped off sharply, and I rode level with treetops. Sunlight splashed the ground, and Cloud kept looking down at the splashes, almost shying. She noticed her shadow, too, curved her neck at the black horse that kept pace with us along the bank, quivered her large, delicate nostrils.

"Hey," I said. "Chill, all right? You've seen your shadow before." I made her stand. After a moment she let out a shivery breath and relaxed her neck a little. We went on.

Beyond the maples I saw cows grazing, beautiful golden Guernseys like Gamp's cow Maybella. "Hi, girls," I called.

The nearest cow raised her head.

Like a bomb going off, Cloud braked, snorted, and went into rapid reverse, rocking me forward onto her neck. "Whoa! Whoa!" I kicked and thumped her sides. Halfway across the road she stopped with a snort like a breaching whale, raised her head, lowered it, trying to bring the cow into focus. I drew a long breath.

The cow shook her head and lumbered closer. Cloud ducked out from under me. I grabbed for mane. Missed.

Broken leg.

No dancing.

Amazing what you have time to think of when you're falling off a horse.

But I didn't fall. I left the saddle, lost both stirrups, and sailed along in midair at the end of the reins. Then I hit the saddle again, scrambling and clutching. Ferns and tree trunks whipped by, the air roared in my ears—

Around the corner came a car.

I twisted the left rein around my hand and pulled harder than I can pull. Cloud's back end slewed sideways. I slid over her shoulder and caught myself with one arm around her neck. We stopped facing the high bank.

The dead leaves spun. Cloud's sides heaved beneath me. After a moment I turned my head. The car had stopped, too. An old man in a feed store cap gazed wide-eyed through the windshield.

I couldn't speak. I jerked my head: Go on! Slowly, hesitating, he continued up the hill.

I groped for my stirrups. Cloud's shoulders were like quivering white marble. Tiny veins stood out on the sweat-soaked hide. I unlocked one hand from the rein to pat her. My hand shook. "I think I might throw up!" I whispered, and a feeble laugh escaped me. Imagine how she'd react to *that*!

It was as if the sky had been torn off. I'd thought I could control this horse's every step, but that had been an illusion. I had no power over her.

Nothing ever scared her at Catamount. Sometimes the roof of the Indoor creaked when the sun came out. Sometimes pigeons flew through, or somebody's pony ran away with her. She might jump or snort then, but usually she just looked.

Now I couldn't even make her walk. She jigged and minced the whole way home. I got a stitch in my side. Everything was a potential cow: garbage cans, chipmunks, stone walls. My hands were hard on the reins; her mouth was hard on the bit. My beautiful dressage horse . . .

Big stump! Cow-shaped stump! She shied in place, rocketing upward, clattering back down in her tracks. I got a death grip on the reins. My eyes prickled with tears. I wanted the Indoor, the windowless, dark, hot building where I was a perfect rider and she was a perfect horse, where there was nowhere to go but around, nothing to see but me, passing in the mirror.

Later that day, in a changing room mirror, I looked at my cotton briefs with the blue and pink ponies on them, my white T-shirt. My legs were pale. My knees were red.

"This would be fun to dance in." Gam handed me something swishy and bright. The fabric felt like the soft skin near Cloud's mouth. I put the skirt on. It hung to my ankles.

The next was blue, gathered at the waist. "Hmm," Gam said.

"Yeah. Like putting a ruffle around a milk crate!"

Gam gave a bark of laughter and then frowned at me in the mirror. "Funny, but not true."

"Yes, it is. I don't *have* a waist!"

She looked over my shoulder in the mirror. "We need a dress."

"I hate dresses."

"That's like saying you hate cheese. Maybe you hate Limburger, but you sure don't hate cheddar!"

I trailed after her up and down the street of our capital city, hunting a dress that wasn't Limburger. Gam looked; I vetoed. Mostly I was back there by the cow pasture with Cloud detonating beneath me. Dressage rider. Ha!

We ended up at the hospice thrift shop. Gam poked impatiently along the rack. "Other people find things here, but I never can."

I can. My school clothes came from stores like this. I turned away from the dark things, the baggy things. In high school I was going to be myself again. If I dared. If I shopped at thrift shops, it would be for jeans.

On a nearby shelf, a patch of blue caught my eye. Some jeans are a better color than others. These were like the lake on a warm, hazy summer afternoon. I unfolded them, and they weren't jeans at all but two lightweight denim dresses. I turned, holding them up. "Ah!" Gam said. "Try them on."

They were soft and comfortable and seemed like they'd always belonged to me. One was narrow and sleeveless and buttoned up the front. It hid my knees. I looked slim, taller, and as if I had a slight waist.

The other dress was the same length but looser and tied in the back, again providing a waist where nature failed to. I didn't look like myself in it either. I looked older, and pretty. If I met somebody who looked like that, I'd think she was pretty.

I looked into that girl's eyes. She looked dazed, as if she'd been knocked down and shouldn't really be standing up yet.

I turned my back on the mirror and climbed into my jeans again. They felt close on my legs now, shutting out the air. Gam paid, and

I carried the dresses out into the sunshine. Even in the bag they felt good, heavy and soft.

"I've got to stop at the Statehouse," Gam said.

The sun glinted off the golden dome. We toiled up the steps, passed the statue of Ethan Allen, and stepped in among the columns, on the gleaming black and white stone floor. A man in a green uniform said hello to Gam. We passed tourists admiring the spiral staircases and walked down the hall between the Senate committee rooms.

The Finance Committee door stood open. The large table in the middle was heaped with papers. Chairs ranged along the walls, where lobbyists and sometimes regular people sat to watch the committee work. At the computer in the corner a young woman looked up. "Hi, Liz! Hi, Mad! How are you?"

"Hi, Tara." Tara Agnoletti was assistant to the committee: small and slim and young, with smart eyes and a nice smile. She worshiped Gam, and she and I liked each other, though we never had a second to talk. Why don't I meet people my own age I like this much? I wondered as she huddled at the desk with Gam.

Sun streamed through the tall window, across the veil of dust that covered the table. In this room the senators argued day after day, in language as dry as your algebra textbook. Here they decided how much tax Mom paid, at the last possible minute every April, and whether we could afford to go to the doctor.

I spent one winter afternoon here among the lobbyists' briefcases, watching. It was too hot in the room, and I nearly fell asleep, but then Gam would speak and I'd wake up. I was trying to see how it was done. How did the Powerful Chair wield her power?

All I saw was Gam listening hard to people who testified, calling colleagues Senator and never by their first names, even though she'd known them for years. She asked a couple of questions, and the lobbyists sat up and listened harder and passed notes to one another. There was too much I didn't understand, and I was glad to walk out at the end of the day. But back here in the room I felt an echo of excitement, and I didn't understand that either.

Gam sat down at the head of the table to sift a pile of papers. I turned to the bulletin board. It was covered with yellowing political cartoons and newspaper articles. Way up in the corner was my sixth-grade school picture, exactly like my eighth-grade picture, except in sixth grade I looked cheeky and confident. I reached for it.

"Hey!" Why do I forget that she notices everything? "Put that back!"

"I hate it." I was about to tear the picture in half, but Gam twitched it out of my hand.

"*I* don't hate it, and it belongs to me!"

"Well, do you have to put it on the *bulletin board?*"

"Yes," Gam said, doing so. "It's to remind me why I'm here."

I hate this speech. "Everything we do is for the children. The children are the future. Someday these children are going to cure cancer, stop global warming, and end war." I always want to say, Hey! Don't leave it all up to us! That's a copout so *you* don't have to solve anything!

But Gam didn't say any of that. She doesn't often. She just looked at my picture and after a moment sighed. "I like a fight too much, Mad. That's my whole problem."

I heard the whirr and click of a camera: Tara, immortalizing another moment in the career of Liz Parker. She lowered the camera and said, " 'It is well that war is so terrible, or we should grow too fond of it.' Robert E. Lee said that."

"Thank you, Tara," Gam said dryly. "Call me when that notice comes in."

We went toward the big door, Gam head down, deep in her own thoughts. I heard the tap of heels on marble, glanced across the floor, and saw a set of green pumps approaching.

"Hello, Liz."

Gam paused and turned. "Hello, Governor."

I looked down, waiting for the introduction. Gam was obsessed with introducing me; she probably thought shaking hands with strangers was therapeutic.

No introduction came. "And this is?" asked the soft, musical voice. I'd heard it many times on the radio, sounding as if it were hung with bells.

"My granddaughter, Madeline." Gam's voice sounded loud, harsh, and flat in contrast. "Mad, this is Governor Hessian."

Now I had to look up and shake the small, soft hand. The governor was no taller than I am, slender, and nearly pretty, with pale blue eyes and lots of light, puffy curls. Were the eyes a shade too close to her nose? Or was the nose crooked? Something was crooked. She smiled, and I caught a glimpse of her narrow bottom teeth, faintly discolored.

"You look *exactly* like your grandmother!" she said, as if it were a thrilling discovery and as if I were five years old. I couldn't help it: I felt that sarcastic point form in my upper lip. "But probably everyone says that," Rachel Hessian said, looking deep into my eyes.

I wanted to squirm away. She stood too close, and I didn't like how well she was reading me. I needed a screen, but I couldn't think of anything to say. After a moment she turned her gaze on Gam. "I envy you senators," she said. "You get to go home and kick back. I have to hang around looking gubernatorial!" She wore, I noticed now, an elegant body-skimming suit of stone-washed silk. Gam glanced down at her culottes and tennis shirt.

"It's a heck of a shame, Rachel! Mad, we'd better get going."

We reached the car. Color burned in Gam's cheeks. Her lips were tightly gripped together.

"Does she always talk in such a teeny-tiny voice?"

Gam's head jerked up. She stared at me for several seconds. Then she let out a crack of laughter that made several passersby turn their heads. "Thank you, Mad," she said. "Thank you. I'm going to remember that!"

8

To: lesismor@v.net
From: madwoman@v.net
Subject: fear

I have fear in my body. I can feel it
making my bones cringe and rattling my
insides, and tell you what, looks like a
giant step backward for the courage-
building project. Guess we'll have to be
failures at high school, too—unless *you*
can carry us.
Cloud shied at a cow...

I hovered over the keys for quite a while, trying to figure out how to tell that story. What's the big deal? Why didn't you ride her back there? Reasonable questions anyone might ask. How could I say how big and scary it felt, her back disappearing from under me, the trees blurring past?

Too hard, and only an hour till dance class.

Delete.

"Gam, will *you* teach me to dance?"

She looked over the tops of her reading glasses. "It's a group activity."

"Well, can you at least teach me the *steps?*"

"I'd rather not, Mad. I'm not the teacher."

"What's that supposed to mean?"

She studied me before answering. Mom does that, too. It usually means trouble. "You wouldn't ask a little girl on a pony to teach you how to ride, would you?"

"If I didn't know anything, I might! Can't you teach me *something*, so I don't look like a total idiot?" I lost control of my voice on the last word; it came out high and quavery.

Gam looked for a moment longer. Then she said, "I'll teach you how to stand."

In the kitchen, under the cold yellow gaze of the Cat, we took positions opposite each other. "Heels together," Gam said. "Let your toes point out naturally, so your feet make a V."

Okay. V.

"You'll dance on the balls of your feet," Gam said, "but anytime you're standing in the set, stand like this. Now I'll show you how to curtsy."

"Am I going to meet the Queen?"

"You'll meet your Maker if you aren't careful! Up on the balls of your feet. Take a small step right, and bring the left foot behind to make a T. Bend your knees slightly; then step back left, and end up with your heels together." She watched me. "Good, but don't look down. 'A Scotsman bows his head to no one,' Morag always says."

"I'm not Scottish, and I'm not a man."

"You had a Scottish great-grandmother, and you have a perfect Scottish attitude: quarrelsome and obstructive! Try again, and make sure you end up with your heels together."

I practiced in front of her, and in my room I dragged the mirror out and propped it against the wall so I could see myself from the waist down. A curtsy looks stupid in pants. I put on the tie-in-the-back dress. My legs had a nice shape when I went up on my toes. L.G. smiled vaguely at them.

"Step, T, bend, step back," over and over until my calves ached. By that time the movement looked smooth and graceful beneath the sweep of the dress.

How would it look in the button dress? I tried it. Neat and crisp.

Maybe I liked the tie dress best.

No, the button—

"Mad, time to go!" Gam called, so the button dress was what I wore.

I sat down in the gym, pretending I wasn't there. If you do it right, no one speaks to you. Never meet their eyes. Look at the floor.

It didn't work with this crowd.

"Mad! Hi!" Gordie said.

"I'm Xenia Marshall. I was in school with your mother," said a lady. I'd be lying if I said I learned her name then, or anyone else's.

Morag arrived with two cases and a CD player. She brought me gillies to try on. "They'll stretch," she said, "so y'want them quite snug."

Gam helped me pick the right size and showed me how to lace them. There seemed to be hordes of spectators—about fifteen by later count. As I bent over my feet, I saw Neil and Sumner come in. I thought very hard about not even *thinking* about the men's room.

A blare of music, quickly quenched, and then Morag said, "Everybody on the floor, please, for fancy footwork."

We all stood in a circle, with Morag in the center.

"Most of our dancing uses the skip-change of step. It starts with a little hop on the left foot."

Everyone hopped, a single, sibilant scuff around the gym. "Y're up on the balls of your feet," Morag said.

Oh. Right.

"As y'hop on the left foot, extend the right."

Hop on left. Forward with right. All one movement.

"Bring the left behind to form a T."

I formed a T. I almost tipped over.

"Forward once again on the right. Now hop on the right, and extend the left. That's the skip-change of step, and it takes up one bar of music. So it's step, T, step, hop, step, T, step, hop—"

All around me I heard the gillies swish, stepping, T-ing, stepping, hopping. I stayed stuck to the floor, as if I'd trod on several gobs of used chewing gum.

Morag gestured with the remote. Music started, and she took my hand. "Forward on the right—step, T, step, hop . . ." I could follow while she was right beside me. Launched on my own, I lost the rhythm.

"Don't swing your shoulders," the masterful voice said behind me. "Hands should be loosely by your sides—and *no scuffing*!" The swish of shoes went abruptly silent.

I can't do this! Lurch, T, lurch, lurch— A twinge in my leg reminded me of my oldest, dearest gym excuse. I stepped out of the circle and stood flexing the knee, watching them all skip by me like a horse show, everyone cantering around the ring. . . .

Cantering! That was what it looked like! The white stallions cantering across the Riding School, light and bold, changing leads every other stride.

I couldn't ride in shows, and I couldn't ride past cows, but as a little kid I spent hours cantering. I should be able to do that.

There was a gap in the circle spinning toward me. I inserted myself. Skip-right, T right, skip-left, T left—

"Aye, you're gettin' it!" Morag said beside me. "Keep a straight leg—don't lift the knee so much. We aren't horses."

Maybe you aren't, I thought, but *I* am!

I was flying now, feeling my way into what Morag meant. I'm used to that. Jane is always telling me to do impossible things. "Suck her back up to your navel, Mad!" Oh, of course! And you do something, you don't know what and you don't know how, and she says, "Yes!"

I was almost sorry when the music stopped. "I got it!" I whispered to Gam. Now *they* would do a dance, and I would practice—

"Take partners," Morag said, "for a simple, easy dance."

Gordie held out his hand. "Would you be my partner?"

"I can't! I don't know how!"

"It's a *class*, Mad! You learn!" He took my hand. His palm was warm and smooth. He led me up to Morag.

She said, "This dance is called Highland Fair." A murmur from the lines that had formed below us, a little groan. I looked down at Gordie's scuffed gillies, making a perfect V. V! I slid my heels together.

"Aye," Morag said, "y'think y're beyond Highland Fair! But it's more of a challenge to do a simple dance well than it is to bash through something harder."

Muted throat clearings from below me.

"Every dance starts with a chord. Gentlemen bow and ladies curtsy." Morag went through the curtsy instructions, and my feet followed. I looked down at my buttons—

"Look straight across at your partner. A Scotsman bows his head to no one."

There's a way of looking at people without really seeing them. Unfocus your eyes; let the other person go soft and blurry. I don't think they notice it, but I'm not sure. I curtsied, Gordie bowed, and I sensed his friendly, confident smile.

Do I bow my head to people? Is that my problem?

Morag said, "The dance begins with the first couple casting off and dancing down behind their own lines for four skip-changes of step."

Was that English? The string of words meant nothing to me. Gordie turned away. Should I follow?

Morag said, "Pull back by the top shoulder." She spun me gently three-quarters around, to face down the line of women. "Off you go, then! Four steps, then turn *away* from your partner, and dance back up."

I thought it was awful when Gam had me in her grip doing that dance on Saturday, but this was worse: alone, wavering off into empty space. Down behind the lines. Back up.

"First and second couples turn by the right hand. To turn—"

They know this! I thought. How can they stand hearing it explained again? I'm ruining their evening.

". . . want the rest of you lot thinkin' this is only for Madeline's benefit. Y've all got a lot to lairn, believe me!"

Gordie straightened slightly. The man beside him shifted and made a face. Was Morag joking? The direct blue eyes looked down the lines, clear and unblinking. "Turn by the right hand."

Gordie took my hand, and we skipped around in a circle, as did the couple next to us.

"And by the left. Look across at your partner." I threw a wild glance at Gordie and then down at the floor again, circling to my place.

"Down the middle, right hands joined, followed by twos."

Gordie skipped me between the lines. I couldn't get in step with him; it felt like a three-legged race.

"Back up, ending in second couple's place, ready for rights and lefts."

Rights and lefts is four people dancing in a square. Cross with your partner, giving right hands. Turn on the side, and give left hands to the person you meet; change places. Cross again with your partner, right hands, and change on the side, giving left hands to end where you started.

When it comes to *doing* rights and lefts, you cross with your partner and turn the wrong way. You stick your hand out to somebody who's supposed to be standing still. He says "No, up!" and you turn in panic. There are people all around you, moving and reaching—and that's just the walk-through, which Morag made us do over and over.

Eventually I was gotten through without mistakes, like a baby "walking" when Mom holds it up by the armpits. Morag turned on the music. Everything smeared in a haze of confusion.

I must have done a few things right, but it felt all wrong, struggling to catch up, catch the rhythm, remember what came next. Arms and hands reaching for me, frowns and smiles, strangers' voices crying, "Up!" and "This way!" The only good thing was that I wasn't embarrassed, even when the hand was Neil's. How can you be embarrassed when you're being hauled into a lifeboat?

Suddenly, while I was poised to cast, the music stopped. I wrenched myself back around. Gordie was bowing, and then everybody except me clapped.

"That was fine for your first dance," Morag said. "We don't expect you to lairn this in half an hour. Y'will progress faster, though, if you listen to the teacher and not to this lot. They don't know as much as they think. Thank partners." She turned back to the CD player.

"Thank you," Gordie said.

"Thank *you*. Excuse me!" I plunged down the hall toward the exit light. I felt jangled, like a broken thermos: The outside looks fine, but inside, you can hear the pieces shifting.

All summer? All *summer* I had to do this?

At the end of the hall I looked back. They were walking through another dance, intricate, braided. Even Neil and Sumner were making mistakes. After a few minutes the music began. I didn't want to like it, but it spoke to my feet. I could hear its language.

"Skip-right, T right, skip-left, T left—" I danced in a circle under the exit light.

9

I AWOKE EARLY the next morning and crept downstairs backward. For some reason that didn't hurt as much. I turned on the computer and sat kneading my calves as it clucked and warmed up.

To: annp@justice.gov
From: madwoman@v.net
Subject: dance

I have to learn 5 kinds of *steps*! Then I have to learn where to go and what hand to use—for *each dance*! There are *thousands of different dances, Morag says!!!*
There are 2 kinds of setting steps, and you use those to *stay where you are*! 2 kinds of steps just for not going anywhere!!!
And I have to go *twice* a week. Morag's starting a beginner class, and she wants me to do both. I think Gam's really too busy, but she says she's going anyway, because a class full of beginners is like a litter of puppies and Morag needs help. Did you know the Powerful Chair is afraid of someone? It's Morag. Me, too!
Was Roxy ever afraid of cows?

I deleted the last line before sending. Roxy was never afraid of cows. They *had* cows when Mom was a kid, and Roxy chased them.

I took out the riding map Mom made for me. At the bottom she'd written "As of Fifteen Years Ago." A spider's web of roads and trails straggled over the paper, dotted with question marks. "Brook here?" "Gate?" "Maybe doesn't connect?"

I drew a cow beside Vesper Road, like a sea serpent on an ancient mariner's map, back when the world was flat. Then I went out to try again.

Where Vesper Road branched off, I took the low road. Cloud clopped along, tense and springy, lightly snorting at every step. The road wound down, and then up again, past the circular driveway and around a corner, where it flattened out between two hayfields. No cows in sight.

The road seemed perfect for a nice trot. The only distraction was a little brick house, with chain-link pens stretching out on either side.

Inside one pen something leaped and barked. Cloud rattled up and down in place.

The kennel. I remembered now; they bred collies. I could hear that high-pitched collie woof. Cloud's ears swiveled. I felt her sink underneath me, ready for rapid reverse.

Could I go wide, through the hayfields? No. All along both sides of the road were square white signs: NO HUNTING, SHOOTING, OR TRESPASSING.

I sat there a long time, looking along the road to its vanishing point. Then I turned back, past Gam's house in the other direction. Cloud jumped every time a chipmunk squeaked. I jumped every time she jumped, snatching at her mouth even when she only stumbled on a rock.

After a few minutes I saw heifers ahead, grazing in a roadside pasture. I turned around before Cloud noticed them.

The world around me stopped looking big. There *were* walls— invisible, wider than the Indoor, but there.

Wednesday Gam woke up with a cold, and I felt a tickle in my throat. I decided to drive it away by mowing the lawn. It would take all day. It would be exhausting. Better not ride.

I filled the mower with gas. I started it all by myself. I pushed it growling into the tall grass, making the lushest, wettest mown lawn smell, chewing up and spitting out small sticks. As the lawn opened up, the place seemed bigger and brighter, and the house stopped looking abandoned. Even the peeling paint didn't seem as noticeable.

It did take all day.

At supper I said, "I don't think I'm up to dancing. How about you?"

"Do you know what Morag does for a living?" Gam asked. "She's a nurse. She comes to class off a ten-hour shift, and she's over fifty!"

"If she's a nurse, she won't want us spreading germs!"

"I will sit hermetically sealed inside the car, and you aren't sick. Are you?"

I could have said I had a sore throat. But it had gone away, and with Gam sitting there red-eyed and croaking, I couldn't pretend.

```
To: lesismor@v.net
From: madwoman@v.net
Subject: 101 ways to fail at dancing

1. Stand there looking stupid while the
dance starts without you.
2. Stub your finger into the place between
somebody's thumb and forefinger when you
reach for their hand.
3. Step on, bump into, trip over fellow
dancers.
4. Forget the difference between Hands
Across and Hands Around. (Across=star.
Around=hoop.)
5. Forget which is right and which is
left.
6-10. Forget how to do the steps. (There
are 5 steps I've been taught so far, 5
ways to mess up.)
Okay, that is only 10 ways, but I've only
been to 2 classes!!
Beginners' class was awful—like a
beginners' riding lesson, except you have
to be the horse and the rider. It's all
one family with Gordie and Gam to help
```

and me to hinder. The family is called
Mackey, and they're there to reconnect
with their roots.
"Roots. Aye," Morag said.

On Thursday morning I rode around the edge of Gamp's old hayfield and found a grassy road leading off one corner.

The road was walled in by dense brush. Cloud walked along it with calm, mild eyes. Even walls of brush made her braver. A partridge flew up with loud wingbeats, and she only flinched. We surprised a deer; I grabbed the front of the saddle when I saw its white tail waving. But the deer ran, and Cloud's only impulse was to follow it. "So what is it about *cows*?"

The road ended in a glade at the bottom of a high rock ridge. Among the trees were mossy stumps. Loggers had been here, many years ago.

It was a short road, barely an hour's ride, round trip. But it was beautiful, and anxiety-free, and if I could get rid of the feeling that I'd wimped out, I might be happy.

When I got home, Gam was at the table, with coffee, the Cat, the newspaper, and a box of tissues. She pushed her hands through her hair when I came in, setting it up in a near Mohawk. "I wish *I* were invisible!"

The newspaper was open to the letters to the editor page. PARKER BETRAYS LOCAL LOGGERS; JOBS BEFORE TREES!; WOODLAND FOR PEOPLE, TOO.

"They're jerks!"

Gam blew her nose. "Yes, some of them. But they're *my* jerks. I've got to look out for them, even when they can't be bothered to know what's going on!"

"Oh." That sounded noble.

"And that was one of the most dangerous and antidemocratic things you've ever heard me say, Mad!"

"It was?"

"Yes. Elitist and patronizing, as if I were a noblewoman looking out for my bunch of peasants!" She sniffed and closed her eyes against that dry, speckly, exhausted feeling we all know so well. "It's their own fault! They don't keep an eye on me, so of course I get that way!"

"So how come you aren't happy now?" I asked, looking at the letters. "I mean, they're keeping an eye on you!"

She shook her head drearily. "Not really. Two of those guys are completely misinformed, and *this* guy"—she tapped PARKER BETRAYS LOCAL LOGGERS—"can't read above second-grade level."

"He had a little help, looks like."

"Especially with his vocabulary!"

"*Will* loggers lose their jobs?" I know what happens when people lose jobs. They have to move, and so do their kids. They can only afford cereal; they live in their cars.

"No. Things will stay the way they are. That was the point. Cut carefully, keep the woods growing, and you keep the jobs. But the Grandcourts won't tell them that, and they won't bother to find out for themselves!"

She sounded so disgusted I had to ask, "Do you like the loggers?"

"Oh, it's the same as any group. I like some, and some I don't. But I don't have to *like* my constituents. They're like family—with one big difference. This I can quit."

What did I just hear? I had a bite of English muffin in my mouth, and it seemed wrong to crunch it. The kitchen was still except for the hum of the refrigerator. Gam sat looking out the window. I saw the sheen of tears in her eyes.

"Rrr-aah?" remarked the Cat, rocketing onto the counter. He started to crunch his kibble.

I chewed and swallowed. "Um, Mom says don't do good deeds just to be thanked."

"Yes. I taught her that." Gam turned away from the window. "Well, I'm sick. Don't mind me."

The phone rang. Gam just sat. On the second ring she said, "Get that, please. I'm not available except to constituents or very good friends."

Third ring. My heart went bump-bumpbump. "But you're here. You want me to *lie*?"

"Say I'm not available. Which is true."

Gam's cold continued all week, and so did the letters. The paper came about the time I was getting back from my tiny little ride. I considered stealing it but didn't, and she always turned to the letters first. I could tell how bad it was by the deep color burning in her cheeks. That couldn't be good for her, first thing in the morning. I'd see her thinking about the letters during the day, too. The color would come up again, and she'd stare off into space.

By Monday two defending letters appeared. They cheered her up a little. To me they didn't seem as well written as the angry ones. The clear-cutters were winning.

But on Tuesday came a letter that made us both happy. "Clear-cutting timber is a wasteful practice with short-term profits for a few and long-term dangers for the rest of us. I voted for the ban, as did five other senators of my party. Anyone attempting to make this seem like a one-person or a one-party issue is either misinformed or malicious. Sincerely, Senator Gordon McIver."

Gam phoned him immediately. "Gordon!" she said in a boisterous voice, the way the football players greet each other when they get on the school bus. Silence. Then she started to laugh, and I realized how little I'd heard that lately.

```
To: lesismor@v.net
From: madwoman@v.net
Subject: bleagh
```

I caught Gam's cold.
You don't want to hear about it. You know all about the throat, and the eyes, and the nose—the poor nose! I've blown it 5,000 times.
The phone still rings, and we let the answering machine answer. I have to study Gam's book so I know her colleagues by name, but I feel too yucky to study.
Unfortunately I didn't get sick till after dancing on Monday.

A Virtual Vacation: That's what I was having. Sit in the kitchen and sniffle and watch my horse graze. Sit in the living room and sniffle and listen to the Powerful Chair on the phone. (The Powerful Chair's cold faded by Wednesday evening, when mine was just getting going.)

I sat over the keys a lot and just tried to be someone, to do something.

My new project: a collection of Gam's political sayings. Like Chairman Mao's *Little Red Book*, she says.

The Powerful Chair's Little E-Book

1. I can't decide which are worse, the evil ones or the stupid ones. (Talking about colleagues.)
2. It's better to have a good enemy than a bad friend.
3. My Yes is Yes and my No is No. But my Maybe is also Maybe.
4. He's a little bit scared of me. (List includes Lt. Governor,

Senate President, House Speaker, 2 members of Legislative Council, at least 6 lobbyists.)

5. It's a very unhealthy life. (See subsection on the food, the all-day sitting, the hot air in the Statehouse [both kinds!], the stress.)
6. What part of No don't you understand?
7. A lobbyist has no permanent enemies and no permanent friends.
8. If I get 8 constituent phone calls on an issue, that's a groundswell. All it takes is a dozen people working together to make a revolution.
9. I love my job. (What she said 2 years ago when the capitol flooded and she couldn't make it in. Not heard recently.)

Glossary:

Constituents. The citizens from the county or district that elected you—whether they voted for you or not.

Constituent service. Answer their phone calls. Answer their letters. If their insurance company won't let their kid get cancer treatment, make phone calls, and phone calls, and phone calls until the company caves. Listen. Try to pass the right laws, which give people what they need, even though you represent all different kinds of people and they need different things. Take the heat because it is impossible to make all these different people happy at once.

Lobbyists. People who prowl the Statehouse trying to make legislators change their votes. They wear wing-tip shoes and expensive suits. They work for anybody who can afford to pay them, and they don't have to tell legislators whom they're working for. They don't even have to tell the truth.

House members represent towns.

Senators represent counties.

The House chamber is big and round with chandeliers and white walls and high windows with lots of little panes. It looks like a temple to Democracy.

The Senate chamber is little and round with etc. etc.

Number of senators completely trusted by the Powerful Chair: exactly 2.

Best (political) friends of Powerful Chair:
Senator Gordon McIver. R. Chairman of Finance Committee back when the Rs outnumbered the Ds. (I don't understand this yet.)
Representative Alice Dybanyk. D. Motives beyond question. If she calls, the PC comes to the phone even if naked in shower.
Representative Jemma Osbert. D. The PC takes a moment to dress before coming to phone.

Political enemies, never to be trusted:
Governor Rachel Hessian. D. The PC brushes hair before answering the phone. Writes down every word said during every phone call. Calls Dybanyk immediately.
Senator Tom Corrigan. D. Other Senator from Barrett County. He and Chair should be allies, but "Tom is ambitious." Wants to be governor or U.S. senator. Needs to show he is different from Chair because she is a woman and he is a man, and because she has been a Senator longer, and because she is smarter and tougher.

Powerful Chair's worst fear:
"Rachel will weasel out of signing the bill."

PC's second worst fear:
"Rachel and Tommy and the rest of the mushy middle will get together and work to repeal the law next year."

PC's third worst fear:
Spiders.

```
From: lesismor@v.net
To: madwoman@v.net
Subject: trail riding

Is trail riding fun? Does Cloud like it?
Should I see if I can bring Brando for a
weekend so we can go out together?

To: lesismor@v.net
From: madwoman@v.net
Subject: strawberries

Our colds are better.
Yesterday we picked 27 quarts of
strawberries. Then we made jam and froze
some and had strawberry shortcake for
supper—just strawberry shortcake! Whenever
I close my eyes, I see strawberries!
Not much trail riding yet—busy!!!
```

I don't call any of that lying. Evading, yes. Leslie would have seen that instantly, if she'd been here.

That's the beauty of e-mail!

The telephone, though not quite as good as a computer, also lets you be invisible and anonymous. Good thing: Gam made me answer the phone most of the time now. I had to find out who was calling and then decide whether Gam was "available" or not.

At first my voice would hardly shape the words: May I ask who's calling? May I ask if you're a constituent? I'm sorry, she's not available right now. Can she call you back later? Not Me. So Not Me.

But gradually it dawned on me; I didn't have to be *me*. I was just a voice, anybody's voice. No one had to know I was a recent eighth grader, standing in a hot kitchen in jeans and T-shirt, with twenty-seven quarts of strawberries on the table waiting to be cut up and the Powerful Chair right there sipping iced tea. I could make myself sound like a secretary, or like that endangered but not yet extinct species, the telephone operator.

"May I ask who's calling?"

"May I ask if you're a constituent?"

"It's Rachel Hessian, Madeline," the sixth caller repeated in her tiny, bell-hung voice. "The governor!"

"Let—let me see if she's available." I pressed my hand hard over the mouthpiece and looked across the room. "It's the *governor*!"

Gam laughed so hard that there was no point in saying she wasn't there. She reached for the receiver. "Hello, Governor! Don't worry, by the time she's voting age, I'll make sure she knows your name!"

"Ga-am!" I know perfectly well who the governor is! I just didn't happen to notice—

"Thank you, Governor, I appreciate the opportunity." Different voice, the courteous voice she uses in dangerous political situations. She was writing down a date and time on her pad. "Thank you, Governor. I'll be there."

"There" was the signing ceremony for Act 88, the clear-cut ban; Gam was the only legislator invited.

"It's bad," Gam said. "She's figured out that she was tricked into this, and she's going to make trouble."

"But she's going to sign it?" If the governor didn't sign the bill, it couldn't become law.

"She'll sign, but she's making it clear that she's signing reluctantly. Inviting me and nobody else shows it's *my* bill, and the timber people should keep up the pressure. Drat!" She sliced into the heart of a big red strawberry, with a quick, restless motion of the knife.

I felt the same. The governor's tinkling voice seemed to rouse all my aggression. "Can *you* invite people?"

"Ye-es," Gam said. "Yes. I should have thought of that. I can't invite anyone officially, but if people happen to show up . . ." She reached for her telephone pad.

I read about the signing in the paper a few days later. The

reporter mentioned the unusual number of legislators present, Ds and Rs alike, and quoted Senator Gordon McIver: "This issue crosses party lines, and that's why I brought my grandson Gordie today. I want him to be able to pass these woodlands and this working landscape on to his grandkids." Pictures of the governor showed a smile strained at the edges, and Gam reported gleefully, "Got her!"

She took me out for pizza; it was the high point of the week.

```
From: lesismor@v.net
To: madwoman@v.net
Subject: How's trail riding?

How's trail riding? How come you don't say
anything about it when you write? Don't
you like it as much as you expected?
See, I know you, Madwoman. I remember when
your mother bought you Cloud, and you were
afraid of her, before you got used to
her. I remember how closemouthed you got.
So anyway, how's trail riding?
```

With the lawn mowed we could see the garden. My cold was gone. I could smell the sweet yellow daylilies, and we weeded until we found them. There were blue and pink cranesbills, a pool of for-get-me-nots, and airy columbines dancing on their tall stems.

We pulled grass, ground ivy, wild morning glory, and brambles out around the plants, leaving the dirt bare and loose. I brought wheelbarrowfuls of cow manure that had aged behind the barn for five years and turned to black, crumbly earth. We dug it in around the perennials, plumped the soil in the bare places. For days every afternoon, the whole afternoon, that's what we did.

I came for this just as much as riding, Leslie! I could have reminded her. Leslie and I agree: Even though she's the Powerful Chair, Gam is an over-the-river-and-through-the-woods kind of grandmother, unlike Leslie's Omi, who's divorced three husbands and wears all three engagement rings while she's working out in a pink-and-purple leotard. I like Omi a lot, but there's something about a grandmother who gardens, bakes, and bird-watches that makes you feel calm, as if there's one thing in the world that's just the way it's supposed to be.

I needed that, and she needed it, too. Something wasn't right. Where was the raw courage that was going to rub off on me? Where were all the skills that I was going to learn?

She kept looking around her kitchen with a sigh and saying, "You have no idea how nice it is to cook for myself again!" During the session she eats breakfast and lunch in the cafeteria and supper at a restaurant. But before she always used to be ready to go out to The Greasy Spoon. I'd been here two weeks now, and we hadn't gone once.

```
From: lesismor@v.net
To: madwoman@v.net
Subject: ???

Check your e-mail!!!
Is the Chair holding you prisoner? Is your
computer down? Have you fallen off and
broken both your arms? So learn to type
with your forehead already and write me
back! Mom won't let me call unless it's
an emergency, and not hearing from you for
five days isn't an emergency—she says!
Now I know how those people on desert
islands feel when they send a message off
in a bottle.
Aleika loaned me a set of hot pink leg
wraps today. They looked fantastic on
Brando. I'll get Mom to buy me some for
Christmas and you get purple for Cloud,
and we'll shock George!
WRITE ME BACK!!!!!
```

When we finally finished weeding, we drove to the farm stand for seedlings. It was nice to roll down the dirt road, listening to the gravel spray against the bottom of the car.

We rounded the corner and saw the heifers. I jumped inside, like

Cloud shying, and my face went hot. Gam didn't know about Cloud's problem. I probably should tell her. I was being secretive again, just like L.G.

But hadn't she and Mom always taught me to solve my own problems?

So what was I doing to solve this one? I couldn't find an answer I respected.

Gam pulled into the farm stand parking lot and just sat there for a minute. Her gaze came back from somewhere far off, and she looked hard at the cars.

"What's the bumper sticker on that truck?"

I craned my neck. "Um, Stoodley for Senate."

She let out a sigh, reached toward her sunglasses in the cup holder, then shook her head and opened the car door.

The farm stand porch was like a rain forest, with brilliant fuchsias and begonias, daturas unfurling like poison trumpets, little orange flowers like dragonflies. There was barely room to walk.

Outside were the plants we'd come to buy: six-packs of petunias, tomatoes, basil, peppers. We'd agreed before coming that we wouldn't let the glories of the porch overcome our judgment. One, maybe two, hanging baskets; that was all. But we lingered in the shade and dense growth, soaking in the color.

"See that man in the straw hat?" Gam was peering out through a gap between plants. "He's turning . . . Thought so!"

"Who is he?"

"He gives a lot of money to my opponents." Coming toward us was an elderly, round-faced gentleman with a boxful of seedlings. "Hello, Alvin!" Gam said, football player to football player.

It took him a minute to recognize her in the dim light. "Hello, Liz! Things lookin' nice around here, aren't they?"

"That they are!" Gam was looking at her list. "Get us a box, Mad— There!" when Alvin was out of earshot. "Did you think he looked smug?"

I didn't know how he looked. I didn't know if the lady in the red shorts had seen Gam and ignored her or just had never glanced our way. I didn't know if the lady behind the counter was standoffish. I did know, answering these questions while we loaded our seedlings into the trunk, that somehow this felt just like school, like conversations you heard in the hall at the end of the day. "Did you see the look Cara gave me?" "Do you think he likes me?"

"I'm here for some weeds!" an old man's voice said behind us. "Replace the ones I pulled up yesterday! What are those weeds called, Mother?"

"Bee balm." A woman's voice, exasperated yet tolerant. Gam and I smiled at each other.

"Fred!" Gam called. "Hasn't she got you trained *yet*?"

"Liz! Well, hello! Haven't seen you since the loony bin let out. Where you been keepin' yourself?"

"I went down a hole and pulled it in after me! Listen, Fred"— she lowered her voice—"you're welcome to come dig up some of my weeds; I've got those dark purple ones, Mary, remember? But buy some here, too, or it'll cost me another vote!"

"Will do, and we'll be over."

"I'll keep a close eye on him!" Mary promised.

We got in the car. Gam gripped the wheel and let out a big sigh. "Well! That wasn't as bad as it might have been."

"No, you didn't embarrass me this time!"

"When have I ever embarrassed you?"

"That time you walked into the grocery store and pulled a U-turn—right around the divider and out the Out door! Everybody was looking!"

"I don't remember that, and anyway, it was two years ago!"

"It was embarrassing. You shouldn't be so paranoid."

"Pot calling the kettle black?" Gam asked sweetly.

I decided not to answer.

At home we hung the fuchsia near the door. I stood under it, and the giant blossoms hung down around me, hot pink and purple. Soon a hummingbird should come.

Cloud grazed out in the pasture. She was getting fat.

```
From: lesismor@v.net
To: madwoman@v.net
Subject: what's going on?

are you mad at me? I can't remember
anything I said or did that would make
you mad—Mad! But when you tell a person,
"I'll e-mail you," and then you stop doing
it—well, that person might get mad. If
they weren't as sweet as me they might.
The last thing I heard was the
strawberries. I don't care about the
freakin' strawberries!
```

Friday it looked as if it might rain. Couldn't ride in the rain.

Early Saturday morning we went bird-watching. I gave myself Saturday off from riding, too.

But it didn't rain Sunday, and Gam is not by nature an early riser, so Sunday I faced failure before seven-thirty. An hour's ride along the trail; a quick excursion to see if the heifers were near the road, which they were; then I was back and unsaddling, and Gam wasn't even up yet, and Leslie's latest message was there when I checked my e-mail.

```
From: lesismor@v.net
To: madwoman@v.net
Subject: enuff already!

I'm not writing to you again till you
write me back! It's either a waste of
time because you aren't checking your
e-mail, or it's a waste of time because
you're being a jerk.
If you get this and you aren't being a
jerk, you might answer.
```

When Leslie says something like that, she means it. I sat at the computer for a long time looking at the message. Then I started typing.

To: lesismor@v.net
From: madwoman@v.net
Subject: sorrysorrysorrysorrysorry!

Sorry.
You were right.
You are always right.
That's why you're my best friend and will
ALWAYS be.
There are cows on Vesper Road. There are
cows on this road. There is a kennel full
of barking collie dogs on this road. I
have one *short* trail I can ride on
without encountering any of these alien
life-forms and sending Cloud into
hysterics.
So here I am. Not riding. Like I always
don't ride when anybody trailers me
anywhere at great expense. What do you
think is wrong with me?
DON'T tell Jane! Just say we're both
enjoying the peace and quiet.
It sure is quiet!

```
From: annp@justice.gov
To: madwoman@v.net
subject: the weather report
It was 98 degrees out yesterday, humid as
the inside of an asparagus steamer.
50 in the office. I had to go out at lunch
and try to buy a sweater. Think you can
find a sweater on your lunch hour in D.C.
in June?
Been here 2 weeks now and know what? It's
easier being a hotshot in a small state
than in a big city.
```

With computers we are leaving no record of our lives for future generations. No letters, no diaries. Our words are evaporating into the ether. That upsets some people.

I think that's the beauty of it—because as history has shown, diaries aren't all that safe! I love the delete key. Say what you like, get it all down; then lean on that key and watch it disappear.

So:

```
It's easier to be a hotshot rider in an
indoor arena, too! Way easier!
I miss you. I miss spaghetti suppers. Gam
likes Mexican—she didn't used to, did she?
She puts cilantro in everything. I hate
cilantro. I bit into a leaf thinking it
was parsley; it's the opposite of parsley!
I miss you yelling at me. I miss your
hair in the morning before you comb it. I
miss bagels. Did you get our strawberry
jam yet?
I miss picking strawberries with you. I
miss hating it and being bored and too
hot and wanting to go over to Leslie's
```

instead. Here picking strawberries is
actually the most interesting thing to do—
because I don't dare ride past those
stupid cows, and riding in circles seems
pointless. Maybe it's always pointless,
but when you live in the country beside a
dirt road, it's easy to tell!
I'm all alone here and outside it's black-
dark, no streetlight—which I love! I love
that!—and the peepers in the swamp across
the road are bellowing and . . .
It's easier being invisible in a crowd
than all alone.

DEL

To: annp@justice.gov
From: madwoman@v.net
Subject: miss you

Did you get our jam?
I rode to the top of the log road this
morning. I saw a deer. Cloud is not
afraid of deer.
I miss you.

When I went on-line to send, Mom's name flashed on my buddy
bar. My heart jumped. A second later the screen split, and her message appeared.

annp: I miss you, too! I keep looking around
for you. I keep starting and thinking, My God!
Where's Mad? I've lost her! I even cry, at night
sometimdelete

"Ha!" Mom was completely confused! She hadn't even hit the
delete key. She'd *typed* "delete," and then she'd hit "enter." Now
a new message appeared on my screen, apparently just as spontaneous and uncensored as the first.

I miss you, too, but I'm having a great time.
Bob at the gym is turning out to be a real
friend, so I have someone to go out with at
night, and that keeps me from missing you *too*
much. He's from New Mexico. He talks slow,
and he seems to have a long horizon to look off
to. So—I'm okay, you're okay?

> **madwoman:** you goofed! Did you know you
> didn't press the delete key? You wrote *delete*
> instead. "Some people would think that was
> a cry for help." Actually—tho I'm *okay!*—I
> reelly reeely miss you! Call me up! There's
> no substitute for the human voice, you used
> to say. E-mail is for geeks, you used to say.
> So who is "Bob at the gym"? The resident
> muscleman?

I went off-line, and a moment later the phone rang. " 'The res-
ident *muscleman?*' He's a computer analyst for the FBI, smarty!"

"Sounds like quite the geek."

"What a mouth you've got on you!" Mom marveled. "This is
your sweet old granny's influence! Is she there?"

"She's at a meeting."

A pause of several seconds. "Have her call me when she gets
home and I will e*vis*cerate her!"

"It's okay! It's only been a couple of hours—"

"It's Sunday night, and it's a quarter to ten!"

"She'll be home at ten. She asked me to go, but I didn't want
to."

"She promised me she'd curtail the political activity this summer
and really spend time with you!"

"She *is!* It's just . . . she's really upset. There's been a lot of trouble about this clear-cut ban."

"Your grandmother *eats* controversy!"

"She's . . . tired. Really tired. She told me she wants to be invisible."
Another long pause. "Terrific! The two of you can trade!"

I felt a little wall of hurt go up for an instant. Mom should be sympathetic, to both of us. Then I saw the momentary flash of headlights against the wall. "Hey, here she is! See?"

"I'll hang up," Mom said. "I'm too frosted to talk with her. How's dancing?"

"Ha!"

I would have liked to tell Mom I hated dancing, and I honestly could have, except.

Except I didn't trust those words at the moment. I loved riding—except right now I hated it because I was stuck stuck stuck.

I hated dancing, except right now I was learning. Two weeks, four classes, and I understood the steps now well enough to practice: skip-change down the dirt road, pas de basque in the aisle of the barn while Cloud finished her grain.

I hated dancing, except. It began with dragging the mirror from the closet and trying on my lake blue denim dresses, the neatly tailored one, the softly flowing one. Who would I be this Monday night? Which costume would I wear?

And if my heart thumped when I walked in the gym door, or contracted, or sank, as my heart has always done when I walk into gyms, that was eased by lacing on the thin leather gillies. My feet filled them perfectly. They made a beautiful black shape. The scallop of the foot, the plump heel, the arch seemed to say something about the steps. Do justice to these feet. Make your Ts; point your toes; touch the foot to the back of the leg lightly, quickly, daintily. Your feet were made for this.

Be transformed. Look at Gam, Morag, Xenia Marshall, wide women, heavy women, solid and slow. They were changed by the music into light, skipping creatures, swift and playful. Sumner? She was there already. But if *they* could change . . .

So I couldn't say I hated it, exactly.

That Monday my head cleared. It was like a car on a cold morning: For a while your breath steams up the windshield, and all at once the defroster is hot enough, and the world ahead looks bright and sparkling. We did a dance called The Machine Without Horses, and for the first time the figures flowed one into another in a beautiful rounded pattern, like turning gears. "Aye," Morag said to me afterward. "That's comin' along!"

"It's a nice dance," I said—as if I could tell one dance from another!

"Aye, it has a flow." Morag looked past me at the rest of the dancers. "Take partners, please, for The Irish Rover."

Panicky looks. There was a rush for the chairs. Gordie vanished down the hall.

When the set was complete, he came back and sat down beside me. We'd danced together a lot by now, but I still didn't know what to say to him. I peeked at the nose he didn't have in kindergarten, the brown eyes that were just the same. We used to sit side by side every day for singalong, and now here we were again.

But Gordie wasn't peeking at me. He was watching Sumner. Among the other dancers she and Neil looked golden and graceful and expressive.

A little *too* expressive! I thought. Hadn't Morag said there were no stars in Scottish country dancing? Sumner sure danced like a star, tilting her head so her fox red tresses flowed, transfixing her partner with her bright-eyed gaze. It suddenly seemed a bit much. Gordie looked perfectly rapt, and I felt my upper lip starting to point.

"So," I said, "if you don't play with trucks anymore, what do you do?"

He started, looking pleased, like someone who's been waiting at a closed door that suddenly opens. "I like farm work. I stay with the Sen—my grandfather a lot in the summer. And in the winter I go snowmobiling."

"Snowmobiling? Yuck!" Uh-oh, I thought as the words tumbled out of my mouth.

"It's fun," Gordie said. "I like it." He didn't seem to care about my opinion. For a second I was relieved, and then I thought, Why *doesn't* he?

"Isn't it destructive? I mean, of the environment?"

He gave me the look I remembered from the sandbox. "No, silly! You're riding on snow! What's it going to hurt?"

I hadn't thought of that. "Well, what about all the exhaust? What about the noise?"

"It's a great way to see the woods," he said. So he didn't have an answer to noise and exhaust! "There's a million trails around here. You can go for miles."

"Do you get all the way over by Gam's?"

"It's not that far over the hill!" That look again. He's a bit of a know-it-all, I thought.

"So you know all the trails probably." My fifth conversational response; in tennis it would be a volley.

Gordie nodded.

"I wish you could show me," I said. "I've only got one trail I can go on without running into cows."

His eyebrows popped up. I felt myself blush.

"If the people on the sidelines would watch and not talk, they might actually lairn something!" Morag announced.

I sat back, hot-faced but almost proud. It had been a long time since I'd been scolded for talking in a class. I watched them dance, everyone moving at once like a swarm of bees. Morag was wrong. I didn't lairn a thing.

At the final chord Gordie turned to me. "What's this about cows?"

I explained, not looking at him. Why didn't you ride her back there? he would ask. Why don't you lead her up to the cows and let her get used to them?

Because I'm gutless, Gordie! I bow my head to everyone, including cows!

"You know what you should do?" he said. (Yes, I know! Yes, I do know!) "You should borrow Elvirah."

"Who?"

"The Sen—my grandfather's pet cow. If she had a cow to live with, she'd get over it, wouldn't she? I mean, I don't know anything about horses, but—"

That seemed like a big admission for Gordie. I jumped in before he could spoil it. "Would he let me?"

"I'll ask."

"Take partners for an easier dance," Morag said.

Gordie held out his hand, and I took it as if I did things like that every day.

13

From: lesismor@v.net
To: madwoman@v.net
Subject: us

Aleika says I'm not as stuck-up as they
thought. Did you think they thought we
were stuck-up? Do you think they think we
think they're dumb? Do you think we're as
dumb to think they're dumb as they are to
think we're stuck-up?
I'm going to the hunter-jumper show with
A. tomorrow.
They didn't know we call them the Club.
They call us the Dressage Queens.

To: lesismor@v.net
From: madwoman@v.net
Subject: The Club

The *Dressage Queens*?
Well, let 'em eat cake!

In fact, smush cake all over their faces! Anything, except go over
to them!

I was beginning to see that I hadn't worried enough about this
summer. It had looked like the light at the end of the tunnel, but
as they say, that light may be an oncoming train! I never dreamed
Leslie would get absorbed into the Club. I thought we'd just miss
each other.

Leslie made friends at her private school, but they felt temporary.
Most of them were going on to private high schools, none had
horses at Catamount, and they were the kinds of friends you sit
with at lunch, not invite home into your life.

Now it was Aleika this, Aleika that. Not that Aleika was horrible.
She was pretty; she was a Clubber; she showed on the hunter cir-
cuit. I'd never seen her do anything mean to her horse, and she
wasn't one of the Club backstabbers. But beyond that, who knew?

Hey, I'm making new friends, too! I thought. I didn't want to go on and on about Gordie, because Leslie seemed to have taken a dislike to him. She called him Gordie the Nose. But he wasn't the only person I'd met!

```
To: lesismor@v.net
From: madwoman@v.net
Subject: beginner class

I call them the Mouse family. There's Papa
Mouse and Mama Mouse and Auntie May Mouse
and the three little Mice—except I think
Everett might be a weasel!
They jump at the opening chord. Every
time. When the music starts, they just
stand still. They look at Morag or Gordie
or me!, wondering what to do. So they're
always a bar behind and they never catch
up.
They don't understand that they're
supposed to catch up, and anyway, when
they're supposed to do the next figure,
they stop and look again. And they say,
"Sorry!" "Sorry!" Even when they're
right!!
Gordie and I are their heroes. It drives
Morag crazy. She thinks if you're
confused, you should ask the teacher. But
you don't, do you? You ask the person
who's next worst. I mean, you don't pick
a popular person to sit next to at lunch.
You pick somebody who won't mind you being
there because they're not so high on the
social ladder themselves.
They're nice, though. The Mice . . .
```

Actually, I never looked at the oldest Mouse girl if I could help it. She'd fallen instantly in love with Gordie and blushed like a fuchsia whenever she touched his hand. Blushes are catching, I think, like yawns. Besides, I felt just the teensiest bit jealous, the way I used to feel when he shared his crayons with somebody besides me.

If I couldn't have Gordie, I would rather have danced with Gam or Morag, but more often than not I got Everett. His sisters seemed to prefer any other partner, and Everett preferred me.

So he was standing opposite me when Morag delivered the nightly lecture. Scottish country dancing was not folk dancing, and we were not to stomp about like a bunch of yahoos. This was the ballroom dancing of Scotland, and it was done with a "military precision."

The Monday class usually greeted this with winces and silent stares. They were all liberal Ds, and the military wasn't in favor.

But Papa Mouse nodded intelligently, as if he understood. Fine, but he can't do it! I thought, and opposite me Everett made a cynical face, like Gam when she talks about the governor.

"It's true," I said. "Look at the Spanish Riding School! That's military!"

"Yeah, but in two seconds she'll give the other speech! 'Don't be afraid. The worst you'll do is make a mistake!' " Everett looked his most weaselly, narrow-eyed and scornful.

"They're both true."

"They can't be. Either it has to be perfect, or it doesn't."

"But when you're *learning*, you get to make mistakes. You can't *start* perfect, or you'd never start anything—"

"The set will please be quiet," Morag said.

I felt my face go red. Scolded for talking with a boy!

Second time this week!

Morag put on the music. I curtsied to Everett, started the half figure of eight around the couple above, and surprised myself by loving it.

Flashing diagonally up the set; a perfect buttonhook behind first man; finishing in Everett's place half a bar too soon; on into the rest of the dance. Next time through I made a wider loop, the way Sumner or Neil would have done, and got there exactly on time. Perfect! I felt ready for more, and there was more, and I did that perfectly, too.

"Some of you've noticed y'can get to your partner's place in three and a half bars instead of four," Morag said when the dance was over. "Y'don't solve this by loopin' out a country mile."

I went red.

"Count your bars," Morag said, slowly and significantly, as if it were a mantra. "Make your steps longer or shorter depending on how far you've got to go. Of course, it helps if you remember where that is!"

Everett smiled his weaselly smile. " 'But don't worry about making mistakes,' " he murmured. " 'That's how y'lairn.' " For a second his narrow eyes made me think of Leslie's.

"Time for refreshments!" Morag announced.

"Then I've got to go," Gam said. Another meeting, to plan a further, public meeting about the clear-cut ban. I was being dropped at Gordie's house by Morag. "And I'll pick you up by ten o'clock at the latest," Gam said.

I'm going home with a boy, Leslie. So there!

We rode home in Morag's pickup truck. Gordie was warm beside me. He made room in the cramped cab by turning sideways and putting his arm along the back of the seat, just brushing my shoulders. I couldn't stop noticing it, but he didn't seem to. He was like Morag in his self-assurance, like another grown-up.

"What are they so afraid of?" he asked—about the Mice, of course. "It's like they don't dare move! They make me think of— I don't know. Chickens?"

Morag said, "Everett's no that bad. If I didn't think it'd cause problems with the family, I'd move him over to regular class."

"Everett! The girls are nice, but Everett's a little worm!"

"I kind of like Everett," I said. Gordie made an astonished noise. "No, Everett's all right. He's . . . funny." I meant to say sarcastic, but I wasn't sure I wanted to admit liking that.

Morag said, "I'm afraid to bring the others into the upper class till they know more what they're doin'. They're just the kind to pick up bad habits."

Like me.

"They're no like Madeline," Morag said, and I looked up quickly. "Aye, Mad. You're a neat dancer, and y'think."

"But I—" I stopped myself.

"Aye," Morag said. "Those big loops. But y'didn't do it again, did you? I saw you countin' your bars. Some people never get that."

That was Jane. All along she was teaching me to dance, though neither of us suspected it. "Get her moving freely forward," was Jane's daily speech. "Then accuracy, accuracy, accuracy! *Straight* lines. *Round* circles. If you get movement and accuracy at the same time, that's a big enough job for anyone. Expression comes later, when you aren't thinking about it."

And that was just exactly Scottish country dancing.

"It's like riding," I said. They were saying something else, and I didn't notice I was interrupting till I'd already done it.

"Aye," Morag said, sounding unsurprised. "Only a dance can't throw you and break your arm! That's what the last horse I rode did to me."

"Did you get back on?" Gordie asked.

"With a broken arm?"

"But you're supposed to get right back on when you fall off a horse. Aren't you, Mad?"

"Only if you can!" I said.

I hadn't been able to picture Gordie's house, but as soon as I saw it, I remembered: split-level, in a clearing at the edge of the woods. You entered through the cellar and climbed the stairs to the kitchen, and his mother was always baking something. Tonight it was biscuits. "Everybody eats strawberry shortcake at nine-thirty at night, don't they?" She sat us down to big bowlfuls.

I looked around the kitchen, expecting to see Gordie's yellow toy dump truck in its usual place. In the old days he fed the dog with it: load the kibble, back up to the bowl, and dump, while

Fiona, the Labrador, drooled. Fiona was fat and gray around the muzzle now and probably got her dog food the normal way.

She snuggled her head into my lap while Mrs. McIver asked about Mom and life in our lakeside city. Gordie's big sister passed through. She was shorter than he was now. She could never pound him and take away his favorite truck the way she used to.

"What do you want to do?" Gordie asked when we'd finished our shortcakes. I looked at the clock. No later than ten, Gam had promised. Almost half an hour to go.

If he were Leslie, we'd go sprawl across her bed and talk or page through tack catalogs or riding magazines. Here there were no horse magazines in sight. Sprawling across the bed was out of the question. No dance music. We were too old for trucks.

"I've been dying for a good game of cribbage," Mrs. McIver said. "Maddie, do you play?"

"I have."

"It'll come back to you," Gordie said as he got out the board. "It ain't rocket science!"

"Says the guy who got skunked last time!" his mother scoffed. I watched her while she shuffled the cards. She was short and dark-haired, pretty, and she took up a lot of space in this kitchen—not her weight, but the way she took over this half hour. Did Gordie mind? I didn't mind. Give us something to do, and it felt as if we were friends. All by ourselves, I had no idea.

But Leslie, I thought. It would be so much easier if he were Leslie.

I liked cribbage, but Gam came before we could finish. We went home to the dark house and the Cat, and after he and Gam had gone to bed, I typed an e-mail, not for sending.

```
Leslie, I miss you. I miss squirting each
other with the hose when George and Nesta
aren't around. I miss Brando. I miss Jane.
I miss being a good rider. I always had
that to fall back on before, and now I
feel like a fake. A good rider would get
past those cows. . . .
```

I miss knowing it was you and me, and the
Club was completely separate. I miss its
never even crossing my mind that you might
go over to them. I miss Aleika being just
the one who looked like she must iron her
long blond hair. I don't *want* her not to
be dumb! I don't want you to like her. *I*
don't want to have to like her, and if
you do, I have to, don't i?

DEL

14

From: lesismor@v.net
To: madwoman@v.net
Subject: Congraduations!!

Aleika says you won the Citizenship Award
at middle school graduation. pretty good
for an invisible person—*some*body knew you
were there!
Aleika says it was totally typical of you
not to be there to get your award. The
principal forgot you were gone and waited
on the stage for you to walk up, so some
people pretended to follow you with their
eyes. Now everybody knows you're
invisible! Actually Al and her friends
thot it was pretty cool.

Right! Aleika was never in any of my classes, so I couldn't say she was ever mean to me. In fact, she said hello in the halls; I always figured that was the long arm of Jane. But think I was cool? Not very likely!

The Citizenship Award was given by teachers. I must have won it during those two months when I made myself look into the eyes of every teacher I met, made myself smile and nod hello. At the end of eighth grade, when invisibility was perfected, it began to scare me. If I smiled and got someone to smile back, that showed I was still there.

That morning there was a girl in a mortarboard on the front page. Gam took one look and crushed the paper to her chest. "What day is it? Mad, what day is it?"

I looked at the calendar. "It's the—no, that's last month." I turned the page. "It's the sixteenth, and you have written—"

"Time? What time?"

"Eleven-thirty."

She collapsed against the back of her chair. "Oh, thank goodness! Do I have anything to wear?"

"Wear where?"

"Middle school graduation. I'm giving out the awards— My hair! How does my hair look?"

"Interesting."

"See you later!" She plunged into the bathroom. "Find me something to wear!"

Her Senate dresses were still in the suitcase, wrinkled and stale-smelling. I found a silky polka-dot dress in the back of her closet. Gam groaned when she saw it.

"Not without a girdle, and I'll have to reef it tight!"

"The only other nice dress is wool."

"All right, the girdle! I swore I'd never wear one again, but thank goodness I had sense enough not to throw the thing away! Go get dressed!"

"*I'm* not going!"

"Oh, *aren't* you?" She turned with the girdle in her hands.

"I didn't go to my own graduation! Why should I go to this one?"

"I need you there in case I faint!"

All the way to the middle school I listened to her breathe. Each inhalation ended sharply, as her ribs came up against the solid wall of the girdle. She looked pop-eyed.

But when she walked through the school door, all sign of discomfort vanished. She seemed to pull a veil over herself; with a smile and a handshake she became Senator Elizabeth Parker, a larger person, representing more than what was seen. The school principal seemed girlish by contrast. She led us to the empty auditorium to wait.

The Barrett Middle School auditorium is steep and dark, and the seats are wooden, with no cushions. They're beautiful, with their simple varnished curves, but Gam shuddered and said, "I'll stand for now. The life of an elected official, Mad, is largely spent in uncomfortable chairs."

I sat, scrunched down. They'd come through the back doors. Maybe they wouldn't see me.

I wondered, in the blank ten minutes, what my life would have been like if we'd stayed here. Would Gordie be my best friend? Would I have learned to hold my head up?

Maybe I'd have been like the Lipizzaners. They're never separated from their classmates. The black foals grow into a gang of gray stallions and are brought to Vienna in a group. The video shows them spilling into the white-and-gilt Riding Hall like the middle school kids behind me now, exploring without human interference. If we hadn't moved, maybe I'd still be as free and bold as I was in kindergarten, as self-confident as those white stallions.

On the other hand, I wouldn't have met Leslie. Would I miss her somehow if I'd never gotten to know her? It seemed I would—

"Senator," said a deep male voice behind me.

Gam turned, and her face lit up. "Gordon!"

A large man in an expensive suit came around the corner of the seats. "How's it going?" His voice was a deep rumble, slow and weighty. Gam stepped close to say something, looking straight into his face. They talked that way for several minutes. Behind me the auditorium filled up, wave on wave of noise, and I looked away from the two senators, trying to seem as if I had no connection to them. They were close enough to kiss.

In the Statehouse people talk like that. The halls are noisy; you have things to say that you don't want everyone to hear. I guess the habit carries over into the real world.

Senator McIver started to turn away, but Gam put a hand on his arm. "Gordon, let me introduce my granddaughter, Madeline."

He shook my hand. His palm was rough, the way I remember Gamp's being, and he looked into my face in a distant, kindly way. "Hello, Madeline."

"Mad was Gordie's best friend in kinder—"

"Hey, Senator!" Gordie bounded up to us, bright-cheeked and breathless. "Hey, Mad, Mrs. Parker—"

"Everyone sit with your homeroom class, *please*," the principal intoned.

"Better go back, kiddo," Senator McIver said.

"In a minute. Senator, Mad's horse is afraid of cows. Could she borrow Elvirah?"

"Who's Elvirah?" Gam asked.

Senator McIver turned red. The rich color in his cheeks made him look startlingly like his grandson. "Old cow I've been keeping around, like a fool. No earthly use. What kind of fence have you got, Madeline?"

"Electric."

"And she can get into the barn? She's used to having shelter in bad weather."

"No one's mentioned this to me," Gam said brightly. "I just point that out."

"*Please* take seats," the principal begged. "Graduation ceremonies cannot begin until you're all in your seats."

Things settled down. Gam read a short set of remarks off the back of an envelope, and Gordie loped up twice to receive awards, including one for citizenship. One more thing we had in common!

Then the graduates walked up as their names were called. I missed this! I kept thinking. Hooray! I missed this! While Gam and Senator McIver sat flashing notes to each other, I watched and guessed what these eighth graders were like. Cheerleader, Loser, Jock, Geek. Popular. Unknown. Middle. Gordie was Middle. Good, I don't trust people who are too popular.

There were three Grandcourts: a girl who looked like a younger, fatter Sumner and two tall boys. One of them had hair like L.G.'s but cut short and lying in curls all over his skull. He had a nose stud, too.

L.G. had sat in these seats once and got his eighth-grade diploma. So had Mom. Was L.G. even then the kind of person who would abandon his wife and unborn child?

What kind of person was that? Somebody Mom could love, once, and she was picky. Somebody *I* could love?

But I don't, I thought. It's important to me to remember that. He left at the very idea of me, and maybe I'd like to impress him someday, but I sure don't love him!

After the ceremony we arranged about Elvirah. She was, Senator McIver explained, the last of his Guernseys, kept when he sold his dairy herd. He and his late wife had nursed her through a broken leg when she was a calf; she was ancient now, and he should have sent her to the slaughterhouse, but he hadn't, and he would lend her to me, provided the pasture was good, the barn was good, and the horse wouldn't hurt her.

"I don't think that'll be a problem!" I said.

On the way home Gam said, "You do keep things to yourself, don't you? I see what your mother means."

"Mmm."

"Your face is so enigmatic. I envy you that." I looked at her, startled. "People can always tell what I'm thinking."

"I don't believe it! *I* can't tell what you're thinking!"

"It's true. I can play my cards close to the vest, but people always know that's what I'm doing."

That I'd seen—or heard. It was a tone of voice that said, I am thinking my own private thoughts. You may know that, but you may not know what the thoughts are. I liked it. It seemed honest. Concealment came all too naturally to me. "I must get it from L.G.," I said.

Gam's eyes widened. "L.G.? Now where did that come from?"

He's always on my mind, down deep, but he must be gone from Gam's. Had she liked him? I wondered, and after a moment I asked.

She didn't answer immediately. "Hard to reconstruct," she said at last. "A lot of water's gone under the bridge since then. I don't 'like' people anymore. I've got to trust them, which takes time, and then be able to work with them, and—oh, a lot of things."

"Yes, in politics! But in the family?"

"In the family it would have been better to hold people to that standard, too! But yes, being as fair as I can at this late date, I did like him. Or at least I thought he was promising."

"Am I like him? At all? Or am I like Mom?"

"You're like you," Gam answered promptly. That was the politically correct answer; I could have predicted it. "If you're like anyone, you're like me."

"I am?"

"Yes. You worry too much what other people think."

Not exactly. I think I scorn other people—most other people. Aleika and the Club are sort of right about me.

"Your mother never had a shy moment in her life," Gam said. "I remember having a lot of theories about how to get her over shyness, because I suffered so much from it as a girl, but I never got the chance. I was so disappointed! Isn't that awful?"

"Pretty bad!"

"But that's why she's upset about you. She doesn't understand what it's like. She doesn't know that when you need to, you'll get over it."

"When did you get over it?" I meant the question to be sarcastic, in view of the sunglasses in the supermarket, the scene at the farm stand.

But Gam didn't hear that. She said, "The state wanted to run a gas pipeline through our farm. Next thing I knew I was standing up in—well, it was the middle school auditorium!, surrounded by people and making some pretty strong remarks to the man who was governor then. I remember time seemed to stop, and I thought, Is this me? And it was. The real me, speaking up for the first time. After that . . ."

"There was no stopping you," I said when the sentence had hung unfinished for a while.

The corner of Gam's mouth lifted slightly. "You know what it is?" she said. "I get mad. I'm so aggressive! Somebody tries something, and before I know it, I'm fighting. When I have to think it out beforehand, I'm as scared as I ever was."

"Leslie and I were wondering," I said. "Are you brave when

you're scared and do it anyway? Or are you only brave if things don't scare you?"

"Yes," Gam said.

"Oh, helpful!"

"Sorry, but it's both. My courage rises out of either love or anger—most often anger. I'll be sitting there with my heart pounding, about to have to say something—"

"Like the teacher's going to call on you in class!"

"Yes. And someone on the other side says something, some little thing that's so wrong or treacherous, and my spirit just *surges*. It's like I'm not me anymore, or like—" She laughed. "Oddly enough, it's like I'm invisible! The fight's the only thing that matters, not me or what other people think of me. And that's the best!"

"But . . . it just happens? You don't make it happen?"

"It just happens. And when it doesn't, you have to grit your teeth and go ahead anyway."

15

SENATOR MCIVER looked different when he hopped out of his pickup in Gam's driveway early the next afternoon: a farmer, shirt-sleeves rolled up, blue jeans sagging.

He opened the back of the stock trailer and disappeared inside. "So, old girl. So." Hooves scraped and thumped, and then he emerged, holding Elvirah snugly by the halter, not restraining so much as supporting her, like a man escorting his elderly mother to church.

She looked like a worn-out Persian carpet thrown over a saw-horse. Her coat was golden velour, and all down her neck it wrinkled when she turned her head, wrinkled with the elegance and beauty of a pair of long gloves.

Gam smiled. "It's been a long time since we had a cow on this place! She looks like Maybella, don't you think, Mad?"

"Look!"

Cloud stood rigid in the middle of the pasture, her neck as high and straight as an exclamation point. She blew out her breath: *whoosh! whoosh!*

"I take her to nursing homes," Senator McIver was telling Gam. "You know, I hate those places! A man works forty, fifty years, and his family can't take care of him? But they like to see a cow come in. Had one old guy—"

Elvirah gave a brusque shove against the halter. Her eyes were focused on the lush grass. "All right, all right!" He led her to the gate, and I opened it. Cloud made an extraordinary sound, like a gasp of outrage. Her tail stuck straight up and fountained over her back.

Senator McIver removed Elvirah's halter and handed it to me. It was warm. Golden hairs clung to it, and a rich, sweet scent. "I brought a fifty-pound bag of crimped oats, and I wrote down how much to feed her. She *can* get into that barn if it rains?" Elvirah plunged her nose into the grass. Cloud bugged her eyes out, circling at a trot. There was a long airborne moment between each stride.

The mailman drove in and bumped his car horn: package for us. Gam went to get it, and when she was out of earshot, Senator McIver asked, "How's she doing?"

I didn't know how much Gam wanted him to know, and I hunted for words that would be both true and cautious. "She's . . . having a nice time gardening."

Smile creases fanned around his eyes. "A Parker answer if I ever heard one! You're good already, kid!"

I am?

"I'm worried about her," he said. "I wish to heck she'd retire so I could, but I don't want to see her run off with her tail between her legs."

"You won't see that."

He shook his head. "When everybody hates you, you can't say just how you'll take it."

He knew too much. I just nodded, and he went on. "She's the best They have." *They*, I knew, were the Ds. "Lot of people have ideas, but when Parker goes for something, she makes it count. She'll lead with it, she'll hold you hostage, she'll blindside you or sneak it through or steal your coalition, but she *never* gives up. She's willing to get hurt if that's what it takes—and They count on that. Christmas, so do We!"

"But—" I said.

"But it does hurt. You put yourself out there. You do ask for it. Still—"

Gam came around the corner. "Thanks for Elvirah," I said.

"I'd like to sit and watch 'em get acquainted," Senator McIver said. "Looks like it's going to be comical. But I've got hay down— Hey, you want to come throw bales around three o'clock, you two? I'm a little shorthanded."

Gam looked a question at me. Gordie might be there, I thought.

And the afternoon would be long. I had to admit the afternoons got long, with just the two of us. I nodded.

"All right," Gam said. "My bale-throwing days are behind me, but I'll drive tractor."

Senator McIver's farm is in the next county, but only fifteen miles away. It's one big hillside, spread with meadows and maple trees. When we got there, no one was at the barn, but up on the field two tractors chugged along. Gordie was in front, raking, and just behind him the Senator baled. Soon they finished and headed back to hook on to the wagons.

I helped Gamp hay when I was a tiny girl. I remember the smell and sitting on his lap while he drove the tractor. I remember his brown arms, dusted with golden chaff.

But I hadn't hayed since, and I certainly didn't "throw" bales. I lugged them, slowly, one at a time. I pushed and heaved them onto the wagon, and I watched Gordie throw them. When you see a hay bale you can barely lift sent sailing through the air, you can't help being impressed.

The sun shone, the hay filled the air with its green perfume, Black Angus cattle grazed on the hillside, and when the hay was all in, and the shadows were long, Senator McIver said, "Time to crack a cold one, Senator?" He brought beers for them, sodas for us, and we sat in lawn chairs, watching the swallows dive. The phone rang inside the house, and Gam said with a smile, "It's not for me!"

Senator McIver sat alertly until the answering machine choked the phone off in mid-ring, then relaxed. "My hired man's gone the next couple of weeks," he said, "and they say the sun'll shine. Any chance I can call on you two again?"

Gam looked at me. I pretended not to notice, looking at the wide blue sky, the broad fields, the clipped lawn, the pole barn with its bright bed of shavings.

"I'll help out," Gam said. "I miss haying. But if Mad wants to, she ought to be paid."

"I'll give her what I give Gordie," the Senator said.

"That's not fair," I said. "I can't throw bales—"

"You'll cost me less than Cliff would, and you're here. There's a pond; you're welcome to swim afterward."

"And the snapping turtles are small this year," Gordie said. "No bigger than garbage can lids!"

There was no way I was swimming. I said yes, though. I had a spacious feeling here. The sky was broad, the horizon stretched far away, and maybe I couldn't throw a bale, but I could do what was needed.

Elvirah conducted herself like a queen, and Senator McIver, like a very nervous captain of the guards. The first words out of his mouth when we arrived to hay in the afternoons were "How's Elvirah?" I wondered how he kept from calling us first thing every morning to find out how she'd slept.

She slept fine. Elvirah was too old to pay attention to anything unimportant; a shocked white horse was certainly unimportant. She left Cloud to get over it, and gradually that happened. One morning when I went out, Elvirah was washing Cloud's face. Cloud's eyes were closed in a dreamy expression; I didn't say anything to interrupt them.

The more relaxed Cloud got with Elvirah, the less friendly she was with me. At Catamount she needed me for every interesting or pleasant thing that happened, every break in the monotony of life in her stall. Here all she needed was the pasture gate opened and to be left alone. No more long sessions where she blew her breath over my face, nudged tenderly to make me scratch her, or dozed with her head over the stall door while I sat reading in the aisle. She was hard to catch and grumpy once I'd caught her, bored with circles and the logging road. All she wanted to do was eat and doze with Elvirah.

Gam said, "When are you going to try her on the road again?"

"I don't know, and it's no good holding your tongue if everybody can see you do it!"

Meanwhile we hayed. It was a hot, sunny week, perfect for drying hay.

It was easy being with the Senator and Gordie, almost like family. The two grandparents talked politics, argued, and gossiped. Gordie and I argued, too, and talked about dancing and sometimes kicked around a soccer ball in the beaten dirt of the barnyard while supper was grilling.

The only part I didn't like was when Gordie went swimming. I did have a bathing suit here at Gam's, but it had been a long time since I'd swum where anybody besides Mom or Leslie and her family could see me. You can't hide your knees in a bathing suit. I had to pretend I was afraid of snapping turtles and get teased about that.

Saturday a friend of Gordie's helped hay. His name was Andy, and supposedly he had been in kindergarten with us, though I didn't remember him. He never said a word around the senators, but he and Gordie did way too much laughing off on their own, and I stayed away. It's a bad sign when you hear boys giggling. Like girls, they're dangerous in groups.

```
From: lesismor@v.net
To: madwoman@v.net
Subject: dancing
```

So is it like riding except no horse?
Aleika is going to camp next week with
the rest of the Club—except for the ones
who go with their families to the ocean
or Europe or something.
When A. comes back, I know she won't be
as nice. They're always so much *more so*
when they come back from camp. So when
she's gone, I'll miss her, and when she
comes back, I won't like her.
Speaking of riding, are you . . . ?

```
To: lesismor@v.net
From: madwoman@v.net
subject: dancing
```

Dancing is *just* like riding—*scary!!!*

But I danced anyway. It's been my fate to fall into the hands of masterful women, from Mom and the Powerful Chair to Jane and now Morag, whose authority was so strong you could almost taste it in the air and who could get you to do impossible things just by telling you to.

At the beginning of Monday's class she said, "We'll be working on figures of eight tonight. Aye, I know, it sounds simple, but y'none of you do it as well as y'might."

A couple of people rolled their eyes. Bet she's talking about you! I thought.

"Count your bars of music," Morag said. "Y'should be exactly halfway on bar four. If you're late, speed up. If you're airly, slow down. The music will help if you listen and *count*."

We danced Corn Rigs: first couple dances a figure of eight around the second couple.

Jessie's Hornpipe: figures of eight around the two people below you.

The Wind That Shakes the Barley: reels of three across the dance—

"*Reels!*" The word squeaked out, unplanned. "I can't do reels!"

"A reel of three," Morag said, "is just a figure of eight. That's all you're going to do, Mad—a figure of eight around third couple's position." She made me walk it, while third couple stood still.

But in a *real* reel everyone is moving, cutting in and out, weaving and braiding and—

"Now everyone walk it," Morag said. "Third couple is doing figures of eight, too. You're all dancing on the same track. So cross down, pass the third man giving right shoulder, and then curve round to follow him."

I couldn't listen. I couldn't look at anyone else. All I could do was follow my imaginary eight, as if it were painted on the floor. When you met someone, did you pass in front of him, or did he pass in front of you? It depended on what position he started in. Morag explained, and I didn't understand.

Still, I did it! I actually walked through my first reel! We walked through and through and through and finally danced, and I did it! I turned the wrong way once and heard Morag saying, way off on the sidelines, "Up the way." And I was able to get right back on my eight.

It felt wonderful!

"You look starry-eyed," Neil said, catching up to me as we walked off the floor. I just smiled. My chest felt airy, as if I'd been singing. I might love this, I thought. It could be that I love this! Courage comes from love, Gam said, and I felt full of something new. It might be courage. I'm full of courage, and Neil is talking to me!

A new set formed, and I thought he would go nab a partner. Instead he sat down beside me. Gordie got Sumner, and Neil sat watching her.

I watched her, too. I always did; I couldn't seem to help myself. Sumner was the one you'd pick as the best if you didn't know anything about it, always graceful, always smiling, the red hair flowing, the wrists impossibly slender, the eyes like emerald chips. And her footwork was precise. Too bad she always had to play the prima ballerina; she could be as good as Morag.

You just hate her because she's pretty! my truthful inner voice pointed out.

I don't hate her, I said back. True, she has everything I want: the looks, the self-confidence, the undivided attention of every male in the room. . . . She danced down the middle with Gordie. He gazed besottedly into her eyes. I wanted him to trip, but he didn't.

The only explanation for what I did next was that I was wearing my tie-in-the-back denim dress, and I'd just danced a reel, something I'd thought was weeks in the future and much, much harder than it had turned out to be, and this person who wasn't exactly me seemed able to do anything. Even claim Neil's attention. "Sumner's so pretty!" I said. "She's my cousin. Did you know that?"

Neil's head snapped around. "What? Really?"

My heart beat rapidly, but my voice came out fine. "A shirttail cousin. Though, who's the shirt, and who's the tail?"

"How is she your cousin?"

"My father was a Grandcourt. Lewis."

"But you're a Parker."

"Mom divorced him." Don't, I thought, but I couldn't seem to stop myself. "He left us—before I was born actually."

"Does he live around here?"

"We don't know where he lives. It doesn't matter; we don't want him back. His nickname was L.G.—for Lewis Grandcourt—but to us it stands for Long Gone." Shut up, Mad! Shut up! "Or we call him G.R. for Good Riddance. B.F., Best Forgotten." Oh, make me stop! I pleaded, opening my mouth again. Nothing came out.

"Wow!" Neil said. He was looking at the dancers again—at Gam actually. Now he looked at me again. "That must be a bummer."

I stared helplessly at him. Something was pressing on my vocal cords. I couldn't speak.

He seemed to realize that after a moment and turned back to watch. The heat of his body burned my bare arm. "Excuse me!" I ducked down my customary hall and fled to the girls' room, where a bright-faced girl in a denim dress stared back at me from the mirror.

Her eyes were wide and blurry. She had one hand clamped over her mouth, like a kidnapper silencing a victim. Too late. Where was that hand when I needed it?

Just as Gam had said, my spirit had surged. A giant surge of stupidity!

It doesn't matter, I told myself. Why should it matter? L.G. was no secret. Why should I care if Neil knew? It couldn't mean a thing to him.

But now I had to go back out there. Morag always says, "If you make a mistake, just get to position to start the next figure." It worked; it calmed you down. Abandon the confusion you're in; go on to the next thing you know. I could do that now, just go sit down. Just wait for the next thing to happen.

When I entered the gym, he was talking with Sumner.

Telling her! Right now he was telling her! And she'd think— what? That I was trying to make myself important by claiming cousinship?

But neither of them even glanced my way. He said something, and Sumner laughed, throwing back her head in the way that showed what a long, lovely neck she had.

Why *wasn't* he telling her? Didn't it seem important? Or did she think it was funny? I looked at him tilting his head, so dashing and attentive, and realized: They're both like that! Both of them! How do they manage to look so perfect, with not a mirror in sight?

It must take hours of practice!

```
To: lesismor@v.net
From: madwoman@v.net
Subject: sumner
```

```
Just back from dancing and guess what?
I'm sick of Sumner Grandcourt! She's
affected and stuck-up and snobby, and she
isn't as pretty as she looks.
```

I hit "send," and Leslie's name throbbed on my buddy bar.

lesismor: Not as pretty as she *looks*? Explain
that one, Madwoman!

> **madwoman:** She *acts* pretty. All these head
> tilts and flirting and laughing . . . And she
> dances in this really exaggerated way. It's
> like it's too perfect. I thought she was really
> good at first, but Morag said, "Aye, she's
> showy." Morag *hates* showy. But people
> think she's pretty.

lesismor: If people *think* she's pretty, and she
acts pretty, and she *looks* pretty, what makes
her *not* pretty? If a tree falls in the forest and
no one hears, did it make a sound? If Neil
thinks she's pretty and Gordie thinks she's
pretty, isn't she pretty enough?

> **madwoman:** Well, you know what? I'm sick
> of Neil, too! So who cares *who* thinks she's
> pretty!

17

To: annp@justice.gov
From: madwoman@v.net
Subject: turtles

Hay again yesterday—can snapping turtles
really bite your toes off? Gordie said so,
but he seems pretty carefree in that pond.
I think if I went swimming, the only
thing grabbing my toe would be him.
How's Bob-at-the-gym?

That was the message I sent in the morning. Just before leaving for beginners' class, I checked my e-mail, and she'd responded.

From: annp@justice.gov
To: madwoman@v.net
Subject: that mouth again!

"Bob-at-the-gym" is right here waiting to
take me out to supper, and he's *fine*! I
think you'll like him.
So why *didn't* you swim?

My big mouth! First I blab to Neil about L.G., and now I reveal my chickenhood. I wouldn't have made either mistake a month ago.

Gam was still in the bathroom. Mom's question just sat there on the screen, looking at me. Answer, I thought. You don't have to send.

To: annp@justice.gov
From: madwoman@v.net
Subject: swimming

I didn't swim because I never "remember"
to bring my suit. Because when my knees
get wet, they turn all red, like burn
scars, so I don't sun myself much—also
because tanning is the ultimate bore!—so
my legs are white . . . and no, none of that

sounds like enough of a reason not to swim in a turtle pond after haying. "A Scotsman bows his head to no one," Morag says. L.G. would understand my being a chicken, but I don't think my Scottish great-grandmother would.

I sat looking at that, while Gam banged around in the bedroom. In a minute we'd have to leave, I for class, she for a meeting.

What the heck! I deleted back to the word *haying* and sent.

So I was going to like Bob? Yike! When Mom had a boyfriend before, I never met him. "He's the kind you go out with, not the kind you bring home," she'd said. But Bob lived in D.C. Pretty hard to bring *him* home!

When Gam dropped me off, Gordie was the only dancer there. "Are you sure the Mouse family's coming?" I asked Morag.

She turned from the tape player. "The Mouse family!"

Mistake! I felt myself turn red.

"Aye," Morag said. " 'Wee, sleekit, cow'rin, tim'rous beastie,/ O, what a panic's in thy breastie!' "

"I shouldn't call them that. Like I'm so brave!"

"Aren't you?" Her eyes were still warm and amused.

"No," I said. "I'm not brave at all."

Her smile seemed to deepen. "Robert Burns has a poem for everyone, I think. Here's one for you, Mad.

> 'Oh wad some power the giftie gie us
> To see oursels as others see us!
> It wad frae monie a blunder free us,
> An' foolish notion.' "

Instinctively I looked down at my dress. No big stain. Nothing unbuttoned. "What blunder? What notion?"

"You figure it out! The Mouse family's pullin' in now."

"To see oursels as others see us." I bent to lace my shoes, thinking: Didn't I do that all the time? Wasn't it my constant mission to remain unseen, unjudged? Hadn't I made a science of it? So what did Morag mean?

"Take hands in a circle, and we'll go over slip-steps."

Like paper dolls, we stood connected, "hands approximately shoulder high." I had Gordie's warm, firm hand and Auntie May Mouse's cool, moist, lax hand.

"Eight to the left and eight to the right, twice." Morag put on the music. We circled.

"To see oursels as others see us." I looked across at Papa Mouse, opposite me in the circle, the one who was seeing me now.

But Papa Mouse was concentrating. The slip-step is simple: Step sideways with one foot; bring the other up to re-form the V. Step close, step close, step close. I made every V precisely. My legs felt strong and springy.

Papa wallowed. He twisted his pelvis, as if trying to go forward and sideways at the same time. His heels never touched each other. He was like a rigid plastic-toy man, being rocked around in a circle by an unseen hand.

Morag stopped the music. "Take partners, please, for a dance."

"Will you dance with me, Mad?" Papa asked. "You're so confident; you always get me through."

What? I felt my eyes go wide. I looked over at Morag. She seemed to be holding back a smile. "Aye," she said as if to herself.

We did a dance called The Linton Ploughman. I let Papa Mouse down badly.

"Do I *really* look confident?" I asked Morag later. She was driving me home because Gam's meeting was in the opposite direction.

"Oh, aye. Y'give the impression of being a much better dancer than you really are."

"Oh. Thanks . . . I guess."

"You're welcome!" Morag said. "That's part of it, y'know. Look like you know what you're doin'. Don't hang your head and blush and apologize every time you make a mistake. You don't do that."

"But I blush all the time!"

"Do you? I never noticed."

I don't believe that! I thought. I can feel my face get hot. But then everybody's face gets hot when they dance. It's hot work, on a warm June night.

Tell me more, I wanted to say. How else do I look?

"Like tonight, though," Morag said, "your partners relied on you too much because y'look sae competent, and you got into trouble."

"Aye—" Oh, no, I was doing it! I was imitating the accent. "I know," I said, hoping it would sound like a stammer. "I let Papa Mouse down—"

Morag laughed out loud. "Papa Mouse! Do y'know what that man does for a living?"

"No."

"He's a steeplejack! He travels all over New England, repairin' these church steeples. I don't even like to think about gettin' up there!"

"I don't believe it! He doesn't dare cast off without written permission!"

"Aye, I know. I used to think the way people dance taught me all about them, but then you get a Papa Mouse!"

Morag dropped me at the end of the driveway. The kitchen light was on, but Gam wasn't back yet.

I walked down to the barn in the almost dark. The peepers' song was fading as we neared July. I could hear Cloud tearing at the grass, the large *whoosh* of Elvirah's breath. I ducked under the fence, and Cloud came to meet me, almost luminous in the twilight. She blew sweet, grassy breath on my face. I shivered, filled with a sense of mysterious communion.

She turned away. I leaned on the gate while the night darkened around me, wondering: If the way people dance doesn't teach you much about them, does dancing teach you much about life? Does it make you braver, the way Gam seems to think? I was doing things I never would have imagined doing, but I still couldn't ride past a field full of cows. What about showing? What about high school?

I went indoors and sat at the computer. "Oh wad some power the giftie gie us . . ." I studied my face in the darkened screen. Portrait of a snub-nosed, brown-blond girl. Dress me right, and I could be Mom. Wrinkle and gray me, and I was Gam. But what *was* I?

Confident. Giving the impression of being a good dancer. Winner of the Citizenship Award . . . What if I really was that person? What would I do differently?

My dreams began to play in my head like movies. Ride for hours cross-country. Compete in dressage shows. Organize a drill team to do Scottish dances on horseback—

What? I didn't know I wanted to do that!

What else?

In high school Leslie and I would be attractive, mysterious figures. We'd set a fashion by wearing riding clothes to school. I'd baffle people with a dozen conflicting explanations for my red knees: Crawled into a fire to rescue a baby. Slid home winning a softball tournament. Injured protesting sweatshop labor—

The telephone rang. I let it, and after some beeps a voice said, "Liz. Tom Corrigan here." Gam's seatmate has a quick voice, with a little stutter that I used to think sounded frank and engaging. "The public forum is a terrific idea—sorry I can't be there. Hey, I hear G-Grandcourt and Sackett held a meeting to plan how to take you out next election. The guy that told me seemed to think you'd be upset to hear that, but I said, 'Y-you don't know this woman!' So . . . good luck! Give 'em hell! We're all behind you!"

"Right!" I said. "Five miles behind!"

I felt all stirred up somehow, and there was nothing to do. I could call Mom, except tonight Gam really *was* late. Better not expose her.

I popped the Spanish Riding School tape—two weeks overdue!—into the VCR and stood watching it, dancing pas de basque steps whenever the music was danceable. The Cat glared and flattened his ears at the sound of my feet.

I half watched the horses, trying to figure out how we *could* dance if we formed a drill team. (And who would be on this drill team? Bill? Nesta? The Club?) Taking hands would be too hard. We'd have to fudge that. But the dances with chase patterns would work, and reels would be perfect. Mirror reels—

All at once I felt myself notice something on the tape. I couldn't figure out what it was at first. I pushed rewind and let the tape move forward again.

Two men worked together to teach the capriole. One, standing beside the horse, held the reins. The other held a long, thin birch whip. At some signal the horse leaped forward. The second man flicked its heels with the whip. The horse kicked out in mid-leap, creating a capriole.

The horse landed, puffing and swiveling his ears, his eyes huge and bright like Cloud's eyes after the cows. The men patted him, and one reached deep down into the tails of his long coat. He brought out a sugar cube. The stallion's ears popped forward. Immediately he was focused and calm, knowing he'd done the right thing.

Focused and calm. Knowing it was all right. Again and again the men reached into their long coattails and brought out the sugar cubes, again and again saying to the stallions, Yes. That's right.

How many times had I seen that? Seventy-five? A hundred? Why had I never noticed what the sugar did? How it claimed the stallions' attention, how it calmed them?

Gam's car pulled into the driveway. After a little delay she came in on a wave of pizza scent. "Hey!" I called. "Do we have sugar cubes?"

It's not a sugar cube kind of house, but once I'd explained, Gam was game to go to the store first thing in the morning. Finally! I could feel her thinking. Finally!

We ate our pizza and drank root beer and played a game of cribbage, and Gam went to bed. I couldn't imagine sleeping. I logged on to the computer. Maybe Leslie was still up.

But the minute I went on-line, Mom's name came up on my buddy bar.

annp: I can't believe it! I was just going to send you XXXs and OOOs. Your knees are not ugly! And even if they were, who cares! You're a fine-looking young woman!

> **madwoman:** I look like a sixth grader. I look like a kindergartner. I look like a better dancer than I am. I won the Citizenship Award at graduation.

annp: you what?

> **madwoman:** I forgot to tell you. But I'm trying to say, I don't look like what I really am—or I'm not like what I look like, or something. I get it from L.G., because he sure can't have been what he looked like! He looks sweet and nice and gentle.

annp: L.G.??? Where'd he come from allofasudden?

What could I say? Two days ago I was showing off to a boy; I used L.G. to get attention. Pretty cheap way to use your absent father!

But I felt as if he was loose now. He was dangerous to me, and I'd better understand.

> **madwoman:** he's been on my mind. He left because you were going to have me, right? So that makes it my fault, only I'm too mature to feel that way—but how *should* I feel? Do you feel anything about him? Is it okay if I ask?

annp: I'm *furious* at him, *still.* It's the silence. If he'd ever said *anything,* or communicated after he left, I could've gotten over it. But he left while I was still loving him. I didn't have any steps to go down. I just fell off the cliff. I still dream about him: romantic teenage

dreams. I hate that! Even when I'm interested
in someone else. I still imagine what I'll say if
he ever shows up. I still want to hurt him
back. For years I knew he wasn't dead because
his mother would have let on. In some way
she'd have told us. But she died 3 years ago,
and lately I have wondered—just a feeling.
You really don't feel anything?

    madwoman: Would he have liked me?

annp: Who knows, baby? Who ever knew
what he liked? When he left us, he wasn't
even twice your age. I thought we were
grown-ups, but it doesn't seem so now.

    madwoman: I'm not like him, right? Not at
    all, right? That wasn't what you meant?

annp: ??? When?

    madwoman: When you said "What are you
    turning into?" The night before we left.

annp: You shouldn't want not to be like him
at all. He could play the guitar. He could
rebuild an engine. He could speak Spanish and
read French. He was beautiful.

    madwoman: Did you ever hate me? Even
    tho it wasn't my fault?

annp: *Never!* Not for one second! It was his
choice; mine were already made. And you
know what? In the end I'm grateful. I got 5
more years living at home, 5 more years with
Dad. That was precious to all of us. He and
Gam were so happy to have us there, so happy
to have *you*. So you got that. If L.G. had
stayed, feeling the way it seems he felt, who
would you be? Someone who'd always known
in her bones she wasn't wanted. Are you all
right? I can get on a plane anytime.

Was I all right? I sat with my fingers on the keys. Two little letters, and Mom would be on her way.

But actually . . . actually, I was fine. Somehow I felt lighter, and simpler, and more safe. Gam was clumping around her bedroom now, squeaking the closet door, thudding the drawer of the bureau—sounds I'd been hearing all my life. L.G. gave me those sounds, just by going. He gave me *this* home, this deep connection. If there were other connections he'd broken for me, I didn't miss them.

annp: Mad?

> **madwoman:**   Lots of guys can rebuild engines. Bob, for instance? I'm fine. Really. I always wanted to ask this stuff, but I never dared because you might cry or get mad or something. This is safer because it's just words on a screen. Like a ouijie board . . . weedja? oudja? eedj't?

annp: Ouija . . . I think. If you're fine, then I'm fine, too, and if you were here, I might cry. Isn't it past your bedtime?

> **madwoman:**   What's the matter with *your* bedtime? Bob shouldn't keep you out so late. But *thank* you! Really!

18

GAM'S IDEA OF "first thing in the morning" is not mine. I had to wait and wait and *wait* while she ate breakfast, delayed by reading the paper, and while she drove to the store.

She wanted to watch. I wasn't sure that was a good idea, but I said yes, and she drove ahead to wait by the cow pasture. I rode after, trying to put on a long-tailed coat of calm.

I watched Cloud's ears. At the place where I'd been turning around—way downhill of the cows—they started to flicker. I said, "Good girl," dug a sugar cube out of my vest pocket, and leaned forward, holding it in the palm of my hand.

Her neck curved like a swan's; her ears zoomed forward. A look of glad surprise came into her eyes, and she swoffled the sugar off my palm.

"Good girl! Walk on."

She walked on, crunching, tipping her ears back at me. In the distance the pasture came into view. The cows clustered under the big trees near the road. Above the solid mass I saw ears twitch, tails swing.

"*Good* girl." Another sugar cube.

As Cloud turned her head, she saw them. She checked, stared, grabbed the sugar cube, and stood wide-eyed, crunching. I almost kicked her to make her walk, and then I thought, No. No hurry. You've got all day. After a long time her head came down a little, and she looked back to check for more treats.

I nudged her with my heels. One step. Before she could stop on her own, I said, "Whoa. Good girl." Sugar cube.

We took a few steps up the road this way and then hit an invisible wall, where her feet rooted to the road.

I dismounted. Cloud relaxed with a sigh. Her head dropped about two feet, and she nudged me. More?

"Not for standing still!" I put the reins over her head and started walking. She walked beside me, head tilted toward my pocket. I gave her another cube, without stopping. Another, another, another. We were getting close. "Whoa." I let her stand and look at the cows, look at Gam leaning on the bumper of her car, look at my pockets full of sugar.

Gam said, "For sheer thrill this is never going to replace rodeo!"

"I've had enough thrill!" More sugar, more steps; without stopping we came right up to the cows. Cloud breathed in their scent, and they looked back in the peculiarly stupid, suspicious way cows have, rolling their eyes and sticking their wet muzzles in the air. "Elvirahs," I said. "See?"

Cloud swung her head away in apparent boredom. More sugar? Time to go do something?

Yes. I got back in the saddle and rode up and down past the cows. Up and down.

Finally I turned in the saddle. "I'm going up the road a piece! See you in a couple of hours!"

Gam said, "Congratulations."

This is the summer I wanted! I thought half an hour later, clopping up the hill. Woods surrounded us, trees reached their upper branches toward one another above the road. Cloud gazed around her, pricking her ears at new sights. She felt soft and relaxed, her old self, her best self.

My heart swelled. What a good horse! All those hours going around and around, with only the brown walls of the Indoor to look at, and she'd stayed so sweet tempered and willing. I hugged her neck. The pommel of the saddle dug into my chest. "I love you!" I whispered, so the trees wouldn't hear.

That was Thursday. Friday I got her past the collies, and the whole world opened up. Now Mom's map was of some use. I was out most of Saturday—I even got lost!—and in the afternoon I made my confession.

```
To: annp@justice.gov
From: madwoman@v.net
Subject: riding
```

It's like when you hurt yourself in front
of people. You don't want them to see it,
and you try not to cry, and your face gets
red—and don't say you don't do that
because I saw when you shut your finger in
the car door that time! What I'm leading
up to is, I haven't been trail riding,
because Cloud was afraid of cows, and I
didn't tell you, because—see above. But
it's okay because now I am, and she isn't.
Have you been e-mailing the Chair? Do you
think she's okay?

Before sending I deleted the last two lines. The Chair hadn't told
on me, and I wouldn't tell on her.

That night we made supper for Alice, Jemma, and Faith. Alice
and Jemma are tall, fashionable grandmothers, members of the
House, and I liked that they didn't assume they were boring me
when they sat at the table telling political stories.

Who knows about this stuff? I wondered. What I was hearing
never got into the papers. Half the public didn't know these
women's names. A good share of the other half thought they were
corrupt, thieving, power-mad, or stupid. No one knew about the
brilliant triple play—Osbert to Dybanyk to Parker—that got the
money for the homeless shelters.

Who would remember in five years? Even two? Here was Faith
with the same stories to tell, and the names of the players were
strange to Jemma, who was newest to politics. Even Gam was
vague about a couple.

It was like war. They did desperately brave things together for
the good of other people, but no one could understand except
those who were there.

Tom Corrigan's name came up, and I told about the message he
left. "That's our Tommy!" Jemma said.

Alice said, "Tom's thinking of going back on us over this clear-cut ban, and he thinks we don't see it."

Gam smiled thoughtfully, the way a fox might smile at a yardful of plump chickens. "Let him think that!"

Jemma said, "When I was a freshman, I was talking with Tom, and your name came up, Liz—did I ever tell you this? And he said, 'Don't go out on a limb for Liz; she'll saw it off if she thinks she needs to!' "

A complex expression overspread Gam's face. "A lot of people believe that."

Faith had been sitting quiet for a while, looking from one face to another. Now she stirred.

"In my first term," she said, "I had a colleague who was brave and smart and everything else I wanted to be. And other senators started warning me about him. 'Watch out. Paul can stab you in the back.'

"I was shocked; it seems to me I was very young then! I kept my eyes open. He was powerful, and he used his power, but I never felt that he betrayed me, even when we were on opposite sides of an issue.

"By the end of my years as a senator I was seeing colleagues keep their counsel around *me*, and I know they said, 'Don't go out on a limb for Faith; she'll cut it off if it's to her advantage.' "

Gam was doodling on her message pad—the outline of a gingerbread woman. As Faith talked, she'd been filling it in, line on line, doubled and braided, until it looked like a woman made of vines or branches. "And was it true?" she asked after a long pause.

"You know the answer to that," Faith said.

Gam sighed. "Yes, I suppose I do."

"It's a funny little world up there," Faith said gently. "You struggle and struggle for the power to be effective, and once you get power, it scares your friends. Or makes them jealous."

"Like middle school!" Jemma said. I jerked in my chair, and Gam gave me a funny look as she added a braided crown to the vine woman's head. "I was a seventh-grade teacher in a former life, and Mad, you wouldn't believe it! The cliques, the gossip, who's popular, who's got cooties—it's just exactly middle school!"

"Except nobody can make you go," Gam said.

Alice and Jemma and Faith looked at one another and looked at me, and none of us said anything for a minute. Then I said, "You know what it makes *me* think of?"

"What?" Gam asked.

"Soccer. Except underneath the game people *think* you're playing there's a secret game, and secret teams, and you're never sure who's on which. Like maybe your goalie's really playing for the secret team."

"That would be Rachel!" Alice said. "And Tommy. Rachel's game is called Get Rachel to Washington, and so is Tommy's because maybe then he'll get to be governor."

"Oh, come on, Alice!" Gam said. "We all want to be governor! All us senators do anyway."

That sounds better! I thought.

Alice and Jemma got up to go. Gam went out with them; Faith and I looked at each other. "Is she—" I couldn't finish. I didn't know what I was trying to ask.

"She's weary," Faith said. "She's feeling all her scars, as if they were fresh wounds. It's quite fracturing, you know. People are always judging you with no knowledge of the inside game, but they're *right* to. If it's not about the real world, it's not worth doing. So . . ." She began stacking the plates.

After a moment I asked, "So?"

"So . . . there are times when everything you do—every meeting, every phone call, every vote—seems to steal a piece of you. You feel hollow. Either you find your spirit again, or you burn out. It would be a very great shame if Liz Parker were to burn out. A great loss."

Hollow: a good word for it. When they yelled "Mad Dog!" in the halls, when they said, "Mad Parker has leprosy," hollow was how I felt.

That was about something stupid, the kind of thing that happens when eight hundred thirteen-year-olds are penned up together. For

Gam it was about important things, like the future of the woods, the continued existence of trees and trails and partridges flying up through the underbrush.

I didn't like to think about Gam's feeling that way.

But over the next few days she seemed cheerful, which may have been a front, and I *was* cheerful.

```
To: lesismor@v.net
From: madwoman@v.net
Subject: !!! *** ^^^ !!!

Those aren't swears; they're fireworks!
I can go anywhere! I can stay out all day
long!! I wish we could go riding when you
come; maybe I'll try to find a saddle for
Elvirah!
Gam says can you come over July 4th?
You'll be able to see dancing; our group
is doing a demonstration in the street
fair. Not me, the good dancers, but
they're dances I can do. We all practice
them.
Leslie, I love dancing! I hate to admit
it, cuz that means Mom and the Chair were
right, but I can't help it. It is like
riding, only better sometimes, because
there's no horse under you having a
different opinion. It's as good as riding
stick horses, or air horses. It's as good
as riding will be when we're really
Dressage Queens. You're going to have to
try it.
```

I could have gone on and on. I loved the flowing patterns and the music, the geometry. I loved the amazement that *I*, *me*, Madeline Parker, could actually do this in front of people and not think about them. I loved that I loved it.

And I loved Morag. I loved seeing her trudge in on Monday night, tired and heavy-footed in thick, cushiony shoes. All day she'd walked from bed to bed to bed. (If I were sick in a hospital bed, would I be glad to see Nurse Morag McAe walk in? Or scared?)

She sat down. She changed out of the sensible nurse shoes into the thin, wicked, black gillies. She stood up ten pounds lighter.

I loved watching her dance. In The Sailor, for instance, most people arrive two bars early for the final rights and lefts and stand there looking like "eedj'ts," as Morag puts it in her tactful way. She herself arrives as if accidentally, as if barely in time, light as a leaf on a stream, *exactly* on the downbeat. All four dancers' hands reach together, all eight feet skip, and for that second the world is what it should be.

Morag's feet make every T and mark every beat of each step. She never misses. She never hurries. When I watch only feet, she seems to be dancing more slowly than anyone else. Her feet *think*.

That Monday night I saw that Sumner's feet don't think yet. If she ever slows down, though, and becomes less self-regarding, she'll get there. Showy dancers, like showy horses, can be smoothed down, maybe more easily than stodgy ones can be gingered up.

I want feet like Morag's, thinking feet. It's the same thing I want from a horse, and maybe I'll get there. After the great cow breakthrough, it seemed I could do anything.

Tuesday I rode, and Wednesday it rained too hard. Gam made arrangements for the big meeting the next day. I sat down at the computer to consider.

How Dancing Is Like Life

1. If you hold your head high and smile, people assume everything is okay, and maybe it will be.
2. You worry that people are watching and criticizing, but mostly they aren't. Like you, they're worrying about how they'll do when it's their turn.
3. Simple, natural, friendly, and helpful: Those are Scottish

dance manners, and they'd be good in real life, too. (How often do you see them?)

4. You depend on the others. If they do well, you do well and the dance is fun. You can't dance if no one else can.
5. You have to be responsible for yourself. Other dancers can help, but they can't dance for you.

What I love best is dancing a whole thirty-two bars without a pause and without a doubt, when the pattern flows and I get there just exactly on time, when I make my Ts and I feel like a good dancer. (This has happened exactly three times so far.)

Names of Figures

Rights and lefts	Grand chain
Ladies' chain	Right hands across
Double triangles	(Left hands back)
Reel of three	Mirror reel
Poussette	Rondel
Allemande	Promenade

Names of Dances

Light and Airy	Davy Nick Nack
Scotland	The Machine Without Horses
The Wild Geese	The Highlandman's Umbrella
Clutha	Merrily Danced the Quaker's Wife
Roaring Jelly	Australian Ladies
The Irish Rover	Mairi's Wedding

Ian Powrie's Farewell to Auchterarder
(I haven't danced all these yet. Some of them are *hard*!)

Most important thing I've learned so far:
A Scotsman bows his head to no one. (I don't bow my head to cows anymore, and that is a Big Step!)

```
To: annp@justice.gov
From: madwoman@v.net
Subject: cilantro
```

It's 6:30 A.M., just me and the Cat awake
here, and guess what?!
The cilantro is in a shrimp cocktail glass
on the windowsill over the sink. The
sunrise was on it when I came down and it
looked so green and like parsley. I thot
yuck! this will be in supper—unless Gam
remembers not to put it in mine, and
tonight she'll forget, because tonight's
the big meeting—
and if she remembers, then *my* food won't
taste as full and spicy as it's supposed
to—
and *then* I thot (don't criticize my
spelling! e-mail is *supposed* to be spelled
wrong!) *then* I thought, I'm going to learn
to like cilantro! Right now! So I ate a
leaf. I didn't brace myself. I just let
the spice go up my nose and guess what?
It's good! I can't wait for supper!
First I'm having breakfast, though, and
then I'm going to riderideriderideride!

We got to the meeting just ten minutes early for two reasons. One, the Chair couldn't find her shoes. Two, she didn't want to stand around talking beforehand. She needed to save her energy for the real thing. At least I think that was why.

The school gym was packed: large people in green and blue work clothes; a sprinkling of young, beaded, feathered persons; khakis and tennis shirts and shorts; and a tree.

The tree, a sack of brown cloth with palmlike cardboard leaves and a face looking out a knothole, moved up and down the aisles, handing out leaflets to anyone who would take one. There were signs reading AX 88 and signs reading ACT 88 SAVES OUR FORESTS.

Senator McIver greeted us at the door, his broad-jowled face inscrutable. "Tough-lookin' crowd," he said. "The ones I know are bad actors, and the rest look pretty scary!"

"There are some friends," Gam said. She seemed quiet, holding herself ready. "Mad, Gordie, where will you be?"

"Right here." Gordie patted the backs of two chairs.

"Good. Don't wander." She looked up at Senator McIver. "Ready, Gordon?" He nodded, and she led the way up to the table in front. I could barely see her, hidden by the Senator's broad back. When she sat down, the microphone obscured her face. I sat beside Gordie, feeling the ache of my seat bones on the hard chair. Saddle sore! Hurrah!

In the middle of the moderator's introduction Faith Hamborough sat down beside me. Senator McIver explained the new law. I didn't listen. If there was one thing I understood, it was the way Act 88 worked.

Then Gam took the microphone. I've heard her speak in public many times, but this time a tremble started deep inside me and spread down my arms and legs. She seemed small and alone. Yes, Senator McIver was beside her. Yes, the moderator was there. But Gam was the one who had made this happen. Gam was the one everybody was mad at. Gam was the one who'd been on hands and knees an hour ago, scrabbling under the bed for her shoes. She seemed perfectly calm; I vibrated like a guitar string.

We needed Act 88, Gam said, because the state had been logged heavily seventy-five years ago. Now hundreds of acres of trees were reaching their prime at once. "We think we'd never do again what we did in the nineteen twenties and thirties. We like to think that we know better. But when I looked into it, I found there were no laws to ensure that. Out-of-state companies wanted to come in and clear-cut. The owners live far away and wouldn't have to live with the consequences. We would. It seemed like time to take precautions."

"Now we'll open the floor for discussion," the moderator said.

First to speak was the tree. He thanked the senators for saving him, so he could shelter the owls, the songbirds—

"The bugs!" someone muttered, not as quietly as he may have imagined. Some people loved the tree; others thinned their lips and looked away.

A man complained about the mess clear-cutting left. When he worked in his woodlot, he used everything, right down to the small branches. He liked to leave things so you could hardly tell where he'd been cutting. Most of the problems with the country could be traced to this kind of waste and mess, and there was plenty of it in state government.

"You'll only get agreement from me," Senator McIver said, trying out a smile.

Now the angry loggers got their turn. They talked about how they'd lose their jobs; they listed the number of kids they were supporting, what local stores they shopped in, how the money they earned and spent helped everyone in town. Gam and the Senator explained, and explained, and explained, as the same questions were asked over and over.

"They aren't listening to the answers," I said to Gordie.

He made a face. "They don't care about the answers! They just want to say their piece. Betcha they're getting paid to. They all work for Grandcourt!"

"How do you know?"

"The hats."

The hats? I looked along the row of disgruntled loggers. Baseball caps, some new, some old and greasy; on the maroon backs were the silver interlaced letters GL. Grandcourt Lumber.

Grandcourts again! I sure didn't feel like claiming them now.

A forest ecologist talked about songbird habitat, and the astonishing number of species you could find in a single square yard of local woods. How trees cool the world and give it oxygen. How the roots of big trees actually draw groundwater closer to the surface, where it feeds springs and brooks, grass and animals and us.

Forests were in trouble all over the world, he said, but here in the Northeast they showed great resilience. Here we could log our woods and keep them healthy if we were cautious.

Gordie nudged me with his elbow. "Look who."

Neil. Standing among the loggers and plain, ordinary, middle-aged people, he looked almost too beautiful. He flipped back the shock of dark gold hair that hung over his eye. "I've got a question for the last speaker. You say we have all this diversity, all this life in the woods. We're told that cutting the trees will destroy this. But these woods were clear-cut seventy-five years ago. Doesn't that prove clear-cut harvesting doesn't do any lasting harm?"

The ecologist rose, looking to the moderator. "May I? Thank you." He turned to Neil. "In a word, no. We have a recovery, but we don't have what we used to. When white settlers came here, this land grew wild strawberries as big as your thumb. We won't get that back. Remember, past logging was done with horses and oxen, not heavy equipment. Big machines compress soil until it's like concrete. It can't hold the water. Rootlets can't penetrate. We don't know what happens to the soil microorganisms. We've never done this before. We have no idea what the consequences may be."

I saw a spark in Gam's eye. She reached for the microphone. "That's something I'm just not willing to gamble on."

Neil's golden cheeks flushed. He sat down. A graying man beside him stood up. "Sumner's father," Gordie said.

Like his loggers and millworkers, Arthur Grandcourt talked about the people he supported, the money he spent in town, and why (not quite in so many words) that entitled him to have his own way in everything. The rumor that the out-of-state buyers planned to clear-cut was unfounded—

"Then why'd they back out when the law passed?" someone asked, in a quiet but carrying voice. Someone else laughed.

But Arthur Grandcourt wasn't finished. "I've seen studies that show the land can recover. There's no proof it can't. There is proof that clear-cutting is the most efficient way to harvest timber, and that means jobs, money flowing in this community, and keeping up our quality of life."

"But—" I heard myself say. Gordie looked at me—not at my face but higher.

At my raised hand.

What am I *doing*? I started to snatch my hand down, and the moderator pointed at me.

Slowly I rose to my feet. My stomach was a lump of ice. I was too scared even to turn red. Dimly, as if at a great distance, I saw the intent look on Gam's face.

"I don't—" I had to clear my throat. "I don't know that much about logging—" What am I going to say? Part of my mind wondered. My voice went on, as if it belonged to someone else. "But isn't this just like how they've overfished the oceans? Everybody said slow down, but they wouldn't. And now there aren't any fish left, and they've all lost their jobs. If you cut down all the trees now, there won't be any to cut later, and there won't be any younger trees growing up. Won't that put loggers out of jobs?"

Sit down now, the separate, calm part of my mind said. I dropped into the folding chair.

Gam and the Senator looked at each other. The Senator reached for the microphone. "Exactly," he said. He didn't sound as if he knew me, had seen me on top of his hay wagons or sprawled in his lawn chair. He just nodded gravely and said again, "Exactly."

I couldn't look at Gordie. Faith Hamborough reached for my hand. Hers felt cool and dry, and not quite there.

Voices blurred on: speaking up for trees, property rights, songbirds, timber sales. I stared at the chair in front of me, the grimy square where a label had been pulled off years ago, and only the gum remained. My pulse pounded in my throat, as if I'd swallowed a little bird.

How did I do that? I don't *do* things like that! I was too limp to tremble now. Couldn't even keep my mouth from hanging open.

A voice brought me back: an old man in worn green workclothes. His voice made my heart ache. The slow rhythm and rounded vowels were like Gamp's and like his friends'. Their talk surrounded me when I was too young to pay attention and they were old enough to call him boy.

"I 'member a toime," the man said, "when all this was open land. I 'member when 'twas a terrible thing, seein' a pasture go back."

Go back. Gamp used to say that. I always pictured weeds, junipers, whipstock saplings, streaking like fire across a hillside pasture.

"Nowadays we know better. Trees keep soil on the hills and hold the water back. I'm old enough I was brought up on stories 'bout the '27 Flood. My folks lived through it. We want to be awful careful we don't let that happen again."

He sat down. People looked at one another. For the first time somebody clapped, and a few others followed suit. A friendly sounding murmur rose like underbrush. Only the maroon-capped group around Neil and Arthur Grandcourt still seemed tense. A few more questions, and it was over. I was astonished to see that we'd been here more than two hours.

People walked past us, talking. Minds had been changed, I gathered. Worries had eased, and the meeting had brought people together.

"I liked what you said," a man said to me. The lady behind him nodded. Other people looked at me as they passed. I wanted to run away.

I didn't want to be seen running away, so I sat.

Gam and the Senator talked with reporters. A radio microphone angled in toward their faces like a curious python. A fat man and a thin blond woman stood close, scribbling as fast as they could in notebooks: eight scrawled words, then flip the page. How many notebooks do they go through? I wondered. When can we go home? "I liked what you said—" Oh Lord!

The gym emptied out. The school janitor wheeled in a long cart and started stacking chairs onto it, with meaningful-sounding clangs. He'd like to go home, too. Gordie went to help him, and I followed, thinking, I'd never do this by myself. I'd stand back and feel sorry for him, but I'd be too chicken.

"We've got 'em started," Gordie said as senators and reporters drifted out the door. We grabbed a few more chairs, then hurried after them.

In the dark parking lot the radio reporter was loading equipment into his van. The fat man roared away on a motorcycle. Gam stretched her arms, and her voice lightened. She said to the woman reporter, "Off the record, Theresa? I'm ecstatic. My expectations were low, but people were terrific. I always forget that."

"We make a pretty good dog and pony show, Liz," the Senator said. "Think we ought to take it on the road?"

"It might not be a—" She stopped walking. She was staring at her car, and I did, too. It looks shorter! I thought. It's—

"Oh, come off it!" Senator McIver said, loud and deep. He wheeled to glare at his pickup. It sat up proudly, tall as ever.

Gam's tires were flat. All four of them.

We stood helplessly for a moment. Then the two McIvers bounded ahead to examine the car. "Now damn it—" I heard the Senator say.

Gam held herself absolutely still for several seconds, the relaxed smile dimming off her face. She drew a long breath, and her expression became unreadable.

"Hey, what's the matter?" the radio reporter asked behind us.

Gam looked at me first, one hard, penetrating look. Then she turned. I had the impression that she weighed more, all at once, that the air was extra still around her.

"I have a few flat tires," she said, and produced a smile that glittered under the streetlight.

The two reporters crowded close. Steve, the radio guy, fished for his notebook and scribbled along with Theresa, glancing at his van from time to time as if he longed for his microphone but didn't dare miss a second.

"I have no idea who could have done it. I don't even want to speculate. We had an excellent meeting here, very civil . . . " She sounded perfectly controlled. My shivering was back.

The McIvers returned. The Senator looked down at me, and put an arm around my shoulders. They know something else, I thought. They're trying not to let the reporters guess.

Theresa said, "I'll just take a look at the car."

"Nothing much to see," the Senator said.

Theresa looked at him sharply. "Then it won't take me long to see it." She headed over, Steve followed, and the Senator shrugged.

"Little extra paint job on the trunk," he told Gam.

Gam closed her eyes. "What does it say?"

"Ax Eighty-eight."

20

To: Leslie? Mom? Me?
Subject: me, of course

Moonlight on the ivory keys. Each key
casts a shadow on the one beside it. My
hands make black spider shadows on the
bookshelf beside the desk.
The flat tires were like puddles of rubber
under the car. Gam locked the kitchen door
tonight for the first time ever. She waited
till I was upstairs where she thought I
wouldn't hear.
My hand knew I was going to speak before
my brain did, and I'm still in pieces. My
voice sounded stupid, like a little kid's,
and I had to clear my throat. Typical! "I
liked what you said," though. Somebody
said that. I liked it, too.
I liked the Senator putting his arm around
me.
I liked—*loved*—Gam in that streetlight,
getting her face on right and saying her
lines. If I could be like Gam, everything
would be all right. Even horse shows. Even
high school.
I learned something tonight. I learned
that big trees pull the water up toward
the surface of the earth, so we can all
drink it.
Something's being pulled up through me.
It's coming to the surface.

Send? Delete?
Save.

*   *   *

The flowers started arriving first thing in the morning. When we got up, two arrangements waited on the doorstep. One was a rearrangement; the Cat likes carnations.

"The funeral's begun!" Gam pulled her robe close to avoid knocking the flowers and went out to the paper box.

The reporter for the local paper was the one who'd left on his motorcycle before we discovered the car. His headline read ACT 88 QUESTIONS ANSWERED and included a picture of the two senators at the microphone. A separate article was titled PARKER'S CAR VANDALIZED and showed the car in front of Cappy's Garage; the painted letters on the trunk were clearly visible. "Cappy must have called him," Gam said. "Drat! I wanted ONE paper to focus on the meeting!"

Over her shoulder I skimmed the meeting article. My own name leaped out at me. My eye flinched from it. For a minute I couldn't look.

When I could, I saw that I was spelled wrong. "Madalyn Parker compared clear-cutting to overfishing, which has depleted the once legendary Grand Banks and put thousands of fishermen out of work—"

"I never said a word about the Grand Banks!"

"Where?" Gam followed my finger. "If you read closely, it doesn't say you did. Our boy is notorious for putting words in people's mouths. You didn't come off too badly."

Maybe not, but being in the paper made my arms and legs feel cringy. It made me feel exposed. Now hundreds of people who weren't even at the meeting knew something about me.

Gam's hand covered the paragraph. I looked down into her eyes. "I meant to say, last night—you were terrific. I was proud."

"You looked scared," I said, feeling my face turn red. "Were you afraid I'd say something stupid?"

"Yes," Gam said. "It's hard to speak in public and make sense when you only have a couple of minutes. You impressed me. Did you have it all thought out?"

"Not even from one word to the next!" I remembered that black void out ahead of my voice. Even now it made me dizzy.

The phone rang, twice, and then the answering machine clicked on. "L-Liz? Tom Corrigan. I'm *shocked* about your car. Are you going to hold a p-press conference? I'll be glad to come. Give me a call."

"Let's get out of here," Gam said. "Breakfast at The Greasy Spoon. I'll call Alice and ask her to drive us."

I love The Greasy Spoon. It's bright and clean and makes the best hash browns in the world. But we'd been dodging the local scene for a month now. Why The Greasy Spoon on this of all mornings?

Everyone was nice. That may have been why. People clustered around our table, shouted greetings across the room. The guy who runs the body shop offered to repaint the trunk for free. "I can't accept that, John, but thank you," Gam said. Five or six people offered the use of their spare vehicles until ours was fixed.

"Cappy says it'll be ready by ten."

"The trunk, too?" I couldn't see Gam driving around in a car that said AX 88.

But she'd brought a grocery bag full of her own bumper stickers—PARKER FOR SENATE, white letters on a Santa red background—and at Cappy's Garage we covered the trunk completely with them. While we worked, the local news blared on Cappy's radio. The car got bigger coverage than the meeting did.

There was Gam, saying again what she'd said last night. "What bothers me most is that I had my thirteen-year-old granddaughter with me. This isn't a side of politics I particularly wanted to show her."

Hearing herself, Gam shook her head. "I sound like a politician!"

"It's true, isn't it?" Alice asked, smoothing out a bumper sticker. "Isn't that what bothers you most?"

"Yes," Gam said after a moment. "But it's at the head of a long list!" She stood back to look at the blazing red-and-white trunk. "This is excessive, isn't it?" Her voice sounded bouncy and satisfied now, keeping Alice and me, along with the rest of the world, at arm's length.

ParkerParkerParker! the trunk shouted. Might as well paint targets on our backs!

The phone rang nonstop for four days: colleagues, reporters, friends, and loyal enemies. Even Rachel Hessian was shamed into calling, after her remark that "Extremism provokes extreme reactions" was published in the papers and *her* phone started ringing. When Leslie e-mailed to say she had a show near us and could I come, Gam said, "Royalton? I hardly know anyone in Royalton! Let's go!"

We got there early. A gray mist hung low over the showgrounds, making the grass seem greener and the world hushed. Gam stopped at the food building and bought a refill for her travel coffee mug.

"Something to eat?" she asked me.

I shook my head. Jane always brings doughnuts.

We crossed the wet grass. The grounds were familiar; this was one of the shows I brought Cloud to last year. I even got her warmed up before I chickened out. I remembered how my heart beat when I told Jane I wasn't going to ride. That fear seemed stronger now than the fear of riding the test. But it couldn't have been, or I would have ridden.

What had I been afraid of?

The ring, with its ankle-high fence of white chain. The judge and the twelve spectators, looking only at me. Forgetting the test. Riding badly.

But I faced Jane! Those blue eyes widening, the words she held back with firmed lips: *Three times* I faced that!

We reached the ring where, according to the schedule, Leslie would soon be riding. A bay horse wobbled through the test. I stood beside Gam, smelling her coffee and watching. The rider saluted the judge and left the ring. Another one entered, to go through the exact same motions. A deep, slow breath seemed to breathe itself through me.

When you aren't competing, a dressage show is just one test, and the next test, and the next test: riders in dark coats and helmets; horses glossy and braided and stiffly well behaved. None of it is up to you. It's like going to the ocean, watching the waves.

Number 42 entered the ring, trotting well. Good test! I started to think, and then I recognized Leslie's style. Her tests always look flowing and spontaneous, as if she were making them up moment by moment just for the fun of it.

Is that Leslie?

She went by me, close. I saw the distinctive shape of Leslie's eyes, that tiny glint of individuality shining through the crack between dark helmet and dark coat.

If *I* couldn't tell that was Leslie, then who could ever tell it was me? I'd be just a black coat, too, just a helmet, just a rider.

Quickly the test was over. Each lasts three or four minutes, like a dance. Leslie halted at the imaginary X in the center of the ring, dropped her right hand to hang at her side, bowed her head to the judges. Then Brando reached down, grabbing all the rein there was. Leslie leaned to pat him, smiling, flushed. With long, loose strides Brando left the ring. I saw Jane walk to meet them.

"Come on, Gam!"

"So this is what you do?" Gam asked.

"This is what I *don't* do."

Leslie was clapping Brando on the neck, the sound muted by her string gloves. "Super!" I heard Jane say.

"Hey!"

"*Hey!*" Leslie said. Her smiling eyes made sunrise curves, narrow and darkly sparkling. When the Cat feels benevolent, he smiles his eyes like that.

I cupped my hand around Brando's muzzle, feeling his velvety heat, hearing Gam and Jane introduce themselves behind us. I said, "You were good! You were *really* good!"

"I know. I couldn't believe it!"

"I didn't recognize you at first," I said. "You looked like anybody till you started to ride. You know what?"

"What?" Leslie looked down on me. After a moment her eyes went round. "No way! You're ready?"

I nodded. "I can do it. I just realized. In September—"

"*Now!*" Jane had turned like a wolf. I hadn't realized they were that close, let alone paying attention. "Put on Leslie's coat and boots," she said, "and get on this horse. I'll get you entered."

My heart felt exactly like a drum: thin, resonating skin stretched over emptiness. In my mind I got into Leslie's boots—too tight—and jacket—too tight—and borrowed breeches from a perfect stranger because Leslie has thighs like paper clips, and Leslie's hairnet and Leslie's helmet—our heads are exactly the same size—and onto Brando, and I was entering at A, working trot sitting—

"No."

"Yes!" Jane said. Gam looked from one to the other of us.

I sensed Leslie above me, holding her breath. Brando sighed noisily and jingled his bit.

"No," I said again, and this time it sounded stronger.

Jane forced a smile. She meant it to be kind, but it looked cynical, a kind of "Yeah, I figured!" smile.

"Hey!" I said. "*I'm* the one who has to ride the test! Not you!"

"Yes, of course."

"I'll ride anytime! In any show near enough for you to come pick me up! But I'll ride my own horse and wear my own clothes. Deal?"

Jane said, "Do you know how much it costs me per mile to drive that rig? I'm not going three inches out of my way without better security than that!"

I felt the heat in my face. Gam half turned and looked into her coffee cup, staying out of this. I said, "I don't break promises!"

"Then don't promise," Jane said. "When I get home, I'll send you a list of shows. You can promise then. Les, take Brando back to the trailer, and let him relax before his next test."

Leslie dismounted, and we walked in silence, on either side of Brando's long neck. He stretched down toward the grass. For horses like ours, who live in barns, the great excitement of these shows is the expanse of green grass. I helped Leslie strip off his tack and sponge his sweat marks away. Then she let him graze.

Why wasn't she saying anything? *I* wasn't talking because my voice would come out wrong. No matter what I said, I was going to sound sulky and resentful. But Leslie could have spoken.

I got doughnuts for us from the box in Jane's cab. We bit, toasted coconut sprayed, and Leslie smiled her eyes faintly at me. Why did she look worried? I put my hand in my pocket and touched the folded newspaper clipping. I'd been carrying it around for days.

Leslie finished her doughnut and slid two fingers into the watch pocket of her breeches. She brought out a piece of paper, unfolded it, and held it toward me.

Same newspaper clipping. She'd bracketed my paragraph in purple ink.

She raised one eyebrow.

I tried to do the same. My eyebrows knitted and squirmed, and Leslie laughed. "Facially crippled! But jeez, Mad! Did you really *stand up*? In front of everybody?"

"Yeah." I felt a smile on my mouth. "It was like I couldn't help it. I had no idea I was going to, and that's how I felt when I saw you riding. I just *knew*: I'm going to do that! I'm ready!"

"You should have," Leslie said. "Before you could think. You still could, you know."

She looked at me seriously, and I felt myself on the verge of saying yes. It was like the time I blabbed to Neil: It felt dangerous, but I wanted to.

But not on Brando. I can ride other horses besides Cloud, but it always takes awhile to adjust. "It's not the way to do it. Wrong horse, wrong boots. I want it to be *right* the first time."

Leslie nodded. "Okay. I can see that."

"So," I said, "have you heard from Aleika?"

"You're mad about her, aren't you?"

I shrugged.

"Three things, Madwoman. Number one, the friendlier I am

with Aleika, the more likely Jane is to give you back your stall. She wants us to mix more, so I'm mixing!"

"Okay."

"Number two, we could use a friend or two in that high school! Aleika's popular. That could help us."

"Oh-kay."

"And number three, I like her. She's not my best friend, but she's nice. I think you'll like her, too."

"All right," I said. "I'll try. But you're going to have to try to like Gordie!"

21

From: lesismor@v.net
To: madwoman@v.net
Subject: July 4th

I can't stay through the weekend! Dad's
poopy aunt is coming, and we have to have
family togetherness! I can come Tuesday
and stay over the 4th and come back
Friday morning.
Isn't it weird having July 4 be on
Thursday? I thot there was a law that it
had to be on the weekend.
Ask the Powerful Chair.
Know what Jane said on the way home? She
said, "I might have been wrong there. What
do you think?" I said—well, I didn't say
anything. I was *flabbergasted*!
(Isn't that a great word? Doesn't it make
you think of thighs?)

To: lesismor@v.net
From: madwoman@v.net
Subject: 4th

The Chair says fine! Tell us when your bus
gets in, and we will meet you!
The Chair says as long as we call it the
Fourth of July it will be held on the
Fourth of July. Announcing that The Fourth
will be held on the second or 5th would
be too absurd even for a politician!
I'm not so sure Jane was wrong. I think
maybe I should have gone for it, even if
the ride was horrible.
Maybe I made a mistake.

Is one mistake so bad?
Dancing teaches you to make mistakes in front of other people,

and laugh about them, and move on. According to the Powerful Chair.

So move on already!

But I couldn't help worrying. When the surge came, was it wrong to turn your back on it? It seemed like it might be. It seemed like I might have hurt myself somehow by saying no.

But it would have been horrible to ride and do badly when I could do so much better on Cloud. That might have made me even scareder.

Jane e-mailed me a list of nearby shows, and I entered in the soonest one, two weeks away. I wasn't taking any bets on whether I'd ride, though. Even though Cloud and I could pass cows now, and collies, and probably even bears, I had that stuck feeling again, and it lasted all the way till Monday's dance class.

Then Morag was there, shedding fatigue and the sorrow that sometimes seemed to hang in the corners of her mouth, as she put on her gillies, as she began to move. And me, too. Me, too.

That night we danced The Duchess Tree, a beautiful slow strathspey that begins with mirror reels. Not just mirror reels, *crossover* mirror reels!

Think of two round fat eights laid flat on the floor, so close that the loops touch at their widest. Three couples dance along these eights, coming in shoulder to shoulder where the loops touch, out again, in again, weaving through each other in perfect synchrony. That's a mirror reel.

When second couple crosses to begin, each partner dancing on the opposite eight, that's a crossover mirror reel.

I watched first, learning by shape, not words. I had to block out Morag's voice, and when the dancers messed up, I looked away, like a mountain climber not daring to look down. When they didn't mess up, it was beautiful, like cables on an Aran sweater, like calligraphy.

Then I got to dance it.

I'll never ride the quadrille in the gold-and-white Hall in Vienna. This might be the closest I'll ever come to that symmetry and freedom. So beautiful to let the loops roll out, to set and circle and cross and cast, and finish up with the angular procession called allemande.

I could tell I was dancing well. I could tell I was good enough. If stout Gam and sturdy Morag and large Xenia looked beautiful, then I looked beautiful, too. Not as beautiful as Sumner, but beautiful enough. I don't know why that dance is called The Duchess Tree, but all through it I kept seeing a large, gracious tree casting shade aboveground, and below it, drawing the silver water up closer to the surface.

"That was grand," Morag said when we finished. Her face glowed. "Now, you *see?*"

Yes. I don't know what Morag meant, but I did see, and I felt our kinship. I looked around to see if anyone else did, but no one had just that look. Gordie, a little bit. But the others just looked warm, and blurry with tiredness.

"Now," Morag said, "white dresses for the demonstration, ladies. Gentlemen, do all of y'have jackets?"

"Not me," Gordie said. He was the newest, youngest dancer on the demo team and a little nervous.

"I'll bring the jacket I used to wear when I was slim," George Marshall said.

"Right enough. Then we'll meet at the bandstand by a quarter to two on Thursday. Mad and Gordie, we'll no be dancin' tomorrow night. The Mi—the Mackeys can't come. You're disappointed," she said to me.

"Aye—I am. My friend is coming, and I wanted her to try it."

"Bring her to the demo, and if she thinks she'd like it, there's a class up your way."

"There *is?*"

"Aye, they have a social in the fall. Your grandmother went last year; did she no stay with you?"

I turned red. Of course she did. I remembered now. But her going to a dance meant nothing to me then.

"I'll give you Phyllis's phone number before y'leave in August," Morag promised.

Leslie's bus got in at ten-thirty the next morning, and the moment she came down the steps, I felt lit with happiness, the way I did when we were third graders and I got to have her over after school. On the way to Gam's we sat in the backseat together, and I'm ashamed to say we giggled every time we made eye contact, as if we were still eight.

Leslie loved Elvirah. Elvirah was indifferent.

"That's what I love! She doesn't need a thing from us!"

"Oh, yeah? Her every whim is catered to! The Senator checks on her twice a week!"

"But she just thinks she deserves it," Leslie said.

Elvirah, on her bed of fresh shavings, blinked at us, burped up a cud, and chewed, with a faraway look.

"She's ruminating! Isn't a cow's stomach called a rumin?"

"I think it's spelled differently." I'd been looking at Elvirah for weeks now and wouldn't have minded going away. But that's the thing about company. They're always interested in something about your house that bores you stiff, and you have to hang around pretending you like it, too.

Leslie likes Gam's pantry, for some reason: the shelves with glass doors, the bins and drawers. She always looks inside them when she visits at Gam's. She likes the Cat, too; Leslie has a thing about indifferent animals.

Fortunately Leslie also liked my room: Larry Mahan, the furniture that can't be moved, the mirror in the closet. L.G.'s picture, which she knew well, got the old familiar questions started, and she pried Mom's answers out of me in five minutes.

"Your mom's so cool. She must have wanted to *kill* him! How could she stand not even knowing where he was?"

"The worst thing was . . . he wasn't who she thought he was. She wouldn't have loved somebody who would do that. So she didn't love a real person. She loved somebody who was making himself up to please people."

"Did she tell you that?"

"Mmm." More e-mails had winked along the wires from Washington over the last two weeks, and that was the upshot.

"Don't you think it's weird that her job now is all about catching people in lies? That's what a lawyer does—"

"And makes them stand up to their obligations. But she was already in law school when he left."

"Yeah, but . . ." We were lying across the two beds, so we could look straight into each other's eyes. "She must have known," Leslie said. "Deep down she must have known. Or maybe . . ."

"What?"

"Deep down maybe he is—was—who she thought he was. Maybe he just made a mistake, and then he was too afraid to come back."

"I don't think so!"

"You wouldn't. That's why—I mean, *imagine* coming back to your mother, after you'd run out on her! I bet even Genghis Khan would think twice!"

We looked at L.G.'s picture. He looked like a boy. Fathers are men. Leslie's father had gray hairs even. "Maybe."

In the afternoon we went haying. "Bring your bathing suit," I told Leslie, and I brought mine.

Leslie was mad because she couldn't throw the bales. "Showoff!" she whispered when Gordie did.

"Maybe he likes you," I whispered back.

"Maybe he'd like a fat lip!" Leslie struggled to push a bale up onto the wagon. Her forehead was sweaty and speckled with chaff, itching, I knew, and making her crosser.

When we finished unloading the last wagon, Gordie said to Leslie, "Want to go swimming?"

"Yes!" I said for both of us, and waited for him to make a comment. But he only said to Leslie, "Every once in a while we see a snapping turtle. If something grabs your toe—"

"If something grabs my toe, I'll drown it!" Leslie made her black eyes narrow as knife blades. "C'mon, Mad, let's change."

We put on our bathing suits in the Senator's gleaming bathroom. We tied our towels around our waists, and mine hung down over my knees. I should have thought of that.

Gordie was already in the pond when we got there. "Come in by where I put my towel," he called. "It's not gooshy there."

We turned our backs to the pond and untied our towels. Leslie glanced over her shoulder. "He's shy," she whispered.

"He is not!"

"He didn't want us to see him in his bathing suit. Trust me!"

The water felt so good. *So* good. "I don't care," I said to myself, surfacing way across the pond. As long as we were haying, I was going to swim, knees or no knees!

I made a tour around the shoreline. When I came back, Gordie and Leslie were treading water near each other, and he was telling her about the meeting.

"Scary! I mean, she was *just* like the Chair!"

"Well, cuter! Don't you think?" Leslie sparkled her eyes at him. This is new! I thought. Maybe Aleika's influence.

Gordie blushed and ignored her. "It made me wonder: Am *I* just like the Senator?"

"Nasally, yes," Leslie said. I don't think he heard her.

"Because—I mean, I don't want to be *just* like him. Although he said to me once, 'Gordie, I know you're a D, and I'm sorry about that, but at least you aren't a moderate.' So that way we're alike. . . ."

Leslie, up to her chin in water, turned toward me and squinted her eyes just a little. Isn't he sweet? she meant. I squinted back: very. Meanwhile underwater I reached for her with my feet. Leslie can't drown me!

At last Gam called, "Girls! Time to go!" We dripped up the bank, the two of us first, Gordie after, all reaching quickly for our towels. My knees were red, the way I'd known they would be. I glanced over and saw Gordie looking at them.

"Wicked skateboarding accident," I said with a perfectly straight face.

His eyebrows went up. "Wow!"

Leslie made a little sound and dived her face into her towel. We dripped up the dirt road to the car and fell laughing into the backseat.

22

AT HOME a strange car was parked in the driveway, and two people stood at the pasture fence.

"Isn't that—"

"Mom!" I wrenched open the car door, ready to run to her.

But who was the man? Would that be Bob? I noticed my wet bathing suit, the towel around my waist, my forearms prickled and scratched by the rough edges of bales. . . .

I let them come to me.

"We didn't know we were coming until this morning!" Mom said after she'd hugged me and printed a dark, wet, bathing suit shape onto her blouse. "We just got in the car at six A.M., and here we are!"

"We" already? I stepped back to check Bob out, then sneaked a peek at Leslie.

She raised one eyebrow. This time it meant: Are they an item? I nodded microscopically, tried raising one of my eyebrows: What do you think? We turned back to Bob.

Dark mustache. Receding hairline. Brown eyes, still and watchful, and a nose with a lot of shape to it, and *little*. He was a little guy, short and lean and so quiet. No extra movements. He'd said only "Hi," in a surprisingly deep, serious voice; but "Hi" is what anyone would say. Leslie gave me a look, a tiny shrug. I shrugged back.

We went up to change. Mom's travel bag was on the floor beside Leslie's bed. L.G.'s picture was on her bedside table. I'd left it on my table, I was pretty sure.

I put on the tie-in-the-back dress and gave Leslie the button one. We looked at ourselves in the closet mirror.

"Dresses," Leslie said. "Who knew?"

I heard footsteps on the stairs. Mom's footsteps. She came to the door wearing her lawyer look, which is pleasant and friendly and unchangeable no matter what happens.

"Leslie," she said, "this is an unexpected treat! Don't worry, I won't kick you out. I can sleep on the couch."

"Why not the guest room?" I asked.

"Bob's sleeping there."

"Oh."

Mom looked at Leslie. "I am going to kick you out now, though. I need a little while alone with Mad. Okay?"

"Okay." Leslie gave me the raised eyebrow again—what goes on here?—and left the room, looking tall in my denim dress. Mom sat down on Leslie's bed and patted the place beside her.

I crossed over to sit on my own bed. I wanted to see her face. "What?"

She picked up L.G.'s picture by one corner and sat looking at it. Her lawyer expression faded, and she shook her head. "I just don't know. . . ."

"Don't know what?"

She looked straight across at me. "He's dead, Mad. All this talk about him— I realized I could probably find out if I wanted to, and Bob helped me, and . . . he's dead."

"Oh." I didn't seem to feel anything. He would be! I was thinking. Here I am planning how I'm going to impress him someday, and all along he's dead. "When?"

"In Honduras, in the big hurricane. There isn't much information, but appearently he got stuck in mud, waist-deep mud, for three days. He was carrying a little girl, and . . . Reading between the lines, it seems he might have been able to save himself alone, but . . . He was sick when the Red Cross got there, and—he died."

"Who was she? Was she his kid?"

Mom shook her head. "It doesn't seem so. When something like that happens, I imagine you pick up whichever child is nearest."

I sat there seeing the TV news pictures: mud, water, a tall man with a blond afro standing in the middle of it, a little girl in his arms. And all the while I kept thinking, Sure! Right! L.G. making himself up again!

"I don't believe it," I said in a thread of a voice. I meant that, but Mom thought it was just an exclamation, or else she couldn't speak, I don't know which. L.G.'s picture fluttered in her hand—jerk jerk jerk—in rhythm with her heartbeat. When I saw that, I did believe. Mom's no fool, and Bob's with the FBI. He must know how to check things out.

"He was right," I said in what was meant to be a hard voice. "A kid really weighs you down!"

And then I *did* feel it, as if it were all my fault.

He ran away from me, but a thousand miles away another little girl caught up with him. Did he think of me, those long hours when his arms ached, and he couldn't sleep, and the mud stank around him? Did he maybe remember that he had a daughter? Did he hold this girl because of me? My tears started to fall. I put my face into the pillow, and after a moment Mom came to sit beside me and stroke the back of my head.

"Does anybody know who she is?" The words didn't sound as if they made it past the pillow, but Mom heard.

"I don't know."

"Could we go down there? Could we find out?"

"If you wanted to, I suppose we could."

I saw us doing that. I saw the wooden cross over L.G.'s bones, and some little girl with dark eyes that he had held, as he never held me.

"I don't know." Maybe we'd adopt her, I thought. Maybe I'd hate her. Maybe she died, too, and it was all for nothing.

The pillow was getting wet, and the pillowcase itched me. I sat up, wiped my eyes with the heels of my hands, sniffed hard. Mom handed me a tissue, and that made me laugh. Don't *sniff*! she always says. "You know what? This is the first time in my life I ever cried about L.G."

She just looked at me. She must have cried about him a lot.

"I'm . . . glad. Not that he died, but— He hung on, didn't he? She would have died if he hadn't hung on."

Mom looked down, her eyes suddenly bright with tears. "Poor

Lewis! He always wanted to be free. I thought we could all be free together, but he didn't see it that way. And then—oh, dear! Stuck in the mud!" She put an arm around me and hugged me to her, hard.

"Don't *sniff*!" I gave her a tissue.

L.G. looked up at me from her hand. I took him away from her. It was her picture, out of her box of abandoned pieces of her life, but I felt as if I owned it. I didn't want to see it now. I opened the drawer of the bedside table and slipped the photograph inside.

"I don't want to call him L.G. anymore."

"It was what everyone called him."

"You just called him Lewis."

"Yes, but— Yes," Mom said. "I called him Lewis."

I heard laughter from downstairs now: Gam and Bob and Leslie, getting along like a house afire. "Are you all right? Can we go downstairs?"

Mom gave one final huge, defiant sniff. "Yes, I'm all right."

We went down, and I found out that quiet, watchful Bob was funny; not jokes, but the deft word or sentence or look that enhanced what the rest of us said and made us funny, too. I saw him watch Mom and seem relieved when he had her laughing. I saw that he was afraid of me, as I was afraid of him, and that seemed right and proper. We should be afraid of each other.

Eventually Mom and Bob went out for steaks, and then Bob made a fire and cooked them. "This is going to seem sexist," Gam said, "but isn't it nice to have a man light the grill? There hasn't been anyone who could light a grill in this family for years!" Leslie and I made a fresh salsa, with lots of cilantro. She was wondering; I could feel it. But I didn't want to cry again, not right before supper, and if I braced, it seemed I could hold it off.

My chest hurt, though, right in the middle. I kept seeing L.G.— the boy L.G., the only one I could see—in waist-deep mud. The hurt got harder and tighter, like something swelling.

"Are you all right?" Leslie's face was close to mine. Her eyes were black and narrow. "What's wrong?" she asked.

At just the thought of telling her my eyes filled with tears. I shook my head and shaped the word *later*. We took the salsa and chips out under the tree.

It was dark by now. The grill glowed, and citronella candles smudged all around to keep off the mosquitoes and the blackflies.

Bugs must have bitten him.

Don't think. Look at Leslie's face. Her lashes are short. They fan out starlike . . .

The little girl must have had—

No. Pay attention. Here. Now. Bob telling Gam just exactly what an FBI computer analyst does—no, not just exactly. He makes it sound more fun, less important, than I'll bet it really is. Mom's eyes can't help shining. Then she can't help looking at me and getting sad. Now *she* is thinking mud and water— No. Pay attention. Here. Now. Ice clinks in our glasses, and the shadows flicker.

I made myself follow every word. Bob had stories about rattlesnakes and reservations, and Mom had met the U.S. attorney general at a party. They wanted to know about Scottish dance, and Leslie's summer of showing, the clear-cut ban and all the ways it rippled through state politics.

"But that won't affect me," Gam said to Bob. "I probably won't run again."

Mom's eyes went big and still. Leslie drew a deep breath and held it. A coal fell in the grill; the glow flared and dimmed.

"Well, don't all look that way!" Gam said.

We all looked down at our laps or plates. I couldn't say I was surprised, but it felt as if she'd just announced she had cancer.

"It's not like I have *cancer*! Look, I'm seventy years old! I'm not having fun anymore, and if I'm not having fun, I don't do a good job!"

"You don't have to justify yourself, Mother," Mom said quietly.

"Like heck I don't! Look at all of you!"

We all sneaked looks around. I saw Bob's mustache curl up slightly.

"I want to be invisible, too," Gam said, "and I can be. In two years nobody will remember there ever was a Senator Liz Parker!"

"We will," I said after a minute. It seemed nobody else was going to say it.

"You'll hate it!" Mom said suddenly. "The first time a tough issue comes up and the Ds wimp out—and they will without you, you know that—you'll be tearing your hair out by the handfuls! You won't be able to *stand* being an outsider."

Gam looked down at her glass. "That's a possibility. Well, it's not a firm decision. I haven't announced it publicly yet, and I'd appreciate all of you keeping it under your hats."

"Does the Sen—Gordie's grandfather know?" I asked.

"No, and my own party has to hear it first. That's very important, Mad."

"I know." The wimpy Ds, the treacherous moderates like Governor Hessian and Tom Corrigan, had first claim on Gam's loyalty, even above that of a firm friend like Senator McIver. Well, she'd be leaving all that behind, too.

"I don't believe she will," Leslie said when we were at last upstairs. The adults had moved into the living room, and their voices were low. Probably Mom was telling Gam about L.G.

"I don't know. She's been weird all summer."

"But it would be like Jane giving up riding!"

"People change, I guess." I would change, too, I thought, if Gam stopped being the Powerful Chair.

I wouldn't like it.

It was actually a relief to change the subject, to tell Leslie about L.G. I didn't cry, though my voice broke once.

Leslie was fascinated. "So he was in Honduras? All this time? Do you think he was a *missionary?*"

More likely running drugs! I thought.

But wait a minute. Wait. Was that fair? "I don't know," I said. "Really, we don't know anything about him."

"That could be nice!" Leslie was thinking about her own father, whose snores and sometimes other bodily sounds rang throughout their house, whose every opinion was expressed even when it wasn't wanted. She knew everything about him, more than enough.

"No!" I said. "It isn't nice!"

But one thing was nice, I discovered, as I lay awake and the hours passed, Leslie breathed in the next bed, and across the hall Bob snored a little. Not bad snores. Not disgusting. I could live with them if it came to that.

I finally *had* L.G. I finally could be proud of him.

He wasn't coming back. He was never going to be proud of me. But he did this one big thing, and I decided it wasn't wrong for me to take comfort from that. I decided over and over, while the moonlight slanted deeper across the bed.

23

MAYBE BECAUSE I hadn't slept much, the morning seemed slow and sticky, like a horse that doesn't want to go forward, like the Mouse family dancing. We all were too careful. There was too much not to talk about, too many worlds suddenly brought together.

Who was I supposed to spend time with? Leslie, my guest? Or Mom? Or Bob, who was probably up here to meet me? We avoided these issues during a long breakfast. Then, abruptly, Mom decided to take Bob for a drive and show him around.

"And now you're mad, Mad!" Leslie said.

"Yeah, but thank goodness!" We had our day back—what we call a grandmother day. Baking, gardening, a slow drive along the dirt roads. We brushed Cloud. We brushed Elvirah. We poked around the barn, looking at the old farm implements and liniment bottles. We made lunch for Mom and Bob when they came back, and around three o'clock the Senator called to see if we could come haying.

"The girls can, but not me. I'm on the radio at seven." Gam listened, holding the phone a little away from her ear; the Senator also has a penetrating telephone voice. He was telling her what to emphasize about Act 88; she nodded without seeming to listen. When he was done, she said, "Now remember, Gordon: no hay tomorrow."

The Senator agreed. Parades, I heard him say. Was he marching in *four*? "How many you doin'?"

"I'm not doing parades this year."

The small, powerful voice exploded. "Whaddya mean you aren't doing parades? How can you not do parades?"

"I'm doing a dance demonstration here in Barrett," Gam said. "Come watch. Gordie's in it."

"Yeah, but how can you not do parades?"

He was still asking when we got to the farm. "How can she not do parades? A politician's *got* to do parades! Is she going to quit?"

How do we not tell him? I wondered. Fortunately it was up to Mom, who had decided to come haying, too, and Mom is a lawyer. I waited for her to come up with the perfect answer.

She didn't have one.

"She *is* quitting! Damn!"

"I didn't say that!" Mom said.

"I got the impression she didn't know what she was going to do," Bob said quietly. "Course I don't know the woman."

"If she knew, you'd be sure of it!" Senator McIver said. "I'll keep my mouth shut awhile. She's as stubborn as a mule if you push her!"

"Thanks," I said to Bob as we all climbed on the hay wagon; the first word I'd directly addressed to him. He smiled at me, reddening at the cheekbones. He's *shy*! I thought. I flashed him a big, bright, encouraging smile, and he turned much redder and looked at his feet. I felt myself turn red, too. Was I coming on too strong?

That was a new one!

We were haying on the highest field, and it was one of those days when the sky is so blue it looks like heaven. We could see for miles out across the mountains, and though it was hot, a breeze was blowing. The Senator's fields and pastures spread themselves below us, divided by stands of big maple trees. Their shade was deep and black and welcome when we passed under, heading down the hill with the first load. We put it in the barn, drank lemonade, and went back for the rest.

Bob could throw bales. Mom had met him at the gym, after all. He looked pretty good in a T-shirt; he didn't seem vain about his muscles, but he'd made sure he had some. Good thing, for a guy that small! He and Gordie and the Senator put the bales on the wagon, and Leslie and I stacked them. With three men loading, they came fast. I looked down on them and thought of mud some-times, flowing mud. Poor L.G. If he'd just stayed here, if he'd stood his ground at the beginning, he, not Bob, might have been on the dry hillside with a bale in each hand.

We wedged the last bale into place and lay on our backs on the load, watching the swallows swoop and dive. Gordie climbed up, and after a minute Mom and Bob. I slid a glance out the corners of my eyes. Were they holding hands? Not yet.

The tractor started, and a moment later a radio voice boomed, loud and distorted. I made out the words *Parker* and *clear-cut* as the tractor putted down the hill.

At the barn Senator McIver parked, hopped off, and reached through a low window. From the old cow barn where the Senator once milked fifty Elvirahs, the radio host's bland voice said, ". . . unpopular in your county. You had your tires slashed recently, you've been the target of angry letters in the newspapers—what's your feeling about all that?"

Gam sounded careful. "I'm always sorry when I have constituents that unhappy with me. But I never win an election by more than three hundred votes. If people are mad, they don't need to slash tires. Get out and vote! I probably shouldn't say this, but you wouldn't need to turn too many people out to be rid of me!"

"See?" Leslie said. "She wouldn't say that if she weren't planning to run."

"That's an unusual admission, Senator!" the radio host said. "My other guest is Senator Tom Corrigan, also from Barrett County, vice-chair of the Natural Resources Committee—"

"We'll stack this load on the barn floor," Senator McIver said. "Won't be able to hear a thing if I run that bale elevator." He and Leslie and I made a bale brigade, passing from hand to hand through the dark barn to the back, where Gordie stacked.

The interviewer said, "Senator Corrigan, you voted for Act Eighty-eight, but in recent days you've joined the governor in criticizing the new law. Can you explain—"

"Yeah, Tommy," the Senator shouted. "Explain why that doesn't make you a treacherous hound!"

Corrigan said, "Steve, as you know a lot of horse-trading goes on at the end of a session. As long as we're making unusual admissions, I'll admit I didn't think hard enough about this one. I voted for it without understanding, and—"

"Then you weren't thinking when you made a speech on the floor in favor of the law, Senator?" Gam said. Pounce! "You said—I'm quoting from the official transcript—you said, 'This is the right thing for the industry and the right thing for the environment, and I'm proud to have had a part in shaping it.' And you did help. We worked together on it. So when you say you didn't think hard enough, I have difficulty understanding what you mean!"

"I can only repeat, Senator, I've changed my mind. I think that's an important thing for a politician to be able to do." Feeble! But was Gam driving him too hard? They belonged to the same party, and the same county, and a lot of people hate to hear a woman sound stronger than a man. They just hate it.

They went a few rounds like that, Gam's tone crisp as a fall apple, Corrigan's voice getting thinner as he floundered for an answer. The Senator seemed pleased; was that a good sign? He was on the side of Gam and the trees, but he did belong to the Other Party.

Suddenly he straightened, a bale in each hand, and stood listening. Tom Corrigan was saying, ". . . agree with the governor. Extreme laws breed extremism. That's why we're working together to make this law less extreme."

"I *knew* it!" The Senator turned to me as if I were a colleague. His voice came from the deepest part of his chest, the way it had that night in the parking lot. "Rachel's going back on us! I said she would! They're going to repeal the law! All right! It's out in the open now, and we can fight!"

But Gam wanted to quit . . . .

On the radio they'd begun taking listener phone calls. The first was Ralph, who called the new law Communist and said that he knew more about the woods than any goldarned senator—

"Is this Ralph LaToye?" Gam interrupted. "Ralph, I'm sure you do know a lot about clear-cutting. Wasn't LaToye Lumber fined last year for spoiling trout streams?"

All right! I thought. She's cookin'!

Gordie said, "You know, she's just like Morag!"

"She's afraid of Morag."

"Everybody in his right mind's afraid of Morag! But I bet Morag's afraid of the Chair, too."

"I don't think Morag's afraid of anything," I said, and as if pushing a button, heard her voice in my mind: " 'Oh wad some power the giftie gie us/To see oursels as others see us!' "

"Who knows?" I said.

"The next caller is Neil, in West Barrett. Neil, you're on the air." Gordie asked, "*Our* Neil?"

"Hello, Senator." Our Neil. My heart double thumped, and my face went hot. I was glad for the concealing darkness of the barn.

"Senator Parker, as you know, the Atlas Paper Company called off a deal with Grandcourt Lumber after your bill passed. As you also know, your daughter was briefly married to a Lewis Grandcourt, who deserted her and her unborn child. Did personal feelings play any role in—"

"Neil," the announcer said abruptly, "that's an inappropriate question, and I'm going to have to cut you off."

A bale thudded beside me. I couldn't pick it up. A hot paralysis swept down my shoulders, down my arms. Gam wasn't answering, she wasn't saying anything, and I knew just how she felt. This is what the word *mortify* means. This is what it's like to die of shame.

Neil. I didn't even like him anymore. I'd just wanted to make him pay attention to me, and almost the minute he had I'd stopped liking him. I should have stayed invisible. I never should have opened my mouth.

I felt Leslie's hand on my back. Mom was coming. A lady on the radio was saying, ". . . say to that last caller: We don't do politics that way in this state! If you want to fight, *fight*, but stick to the issues! Liz, I've watched you a long time, and I haven't always agreed with you, but I respect you, and I'm grateful for the chance to say so."

"And that's all we have time for," the interviewer said in a wilting voice. "I want to thank—"

The Senator made a long arm through the barn window and

snapped the radio off. In the sudden ringing silence he said, "I don't care what party she belongs to. I want that woman to run for governor!"

Then Mom was there with an arm around my shoulders, turning me away from everybody. "Mad? What's wrong?"

"I told him." I could only whisper. "He wouldn't even know if it wasn't for me!"

"It's common knowledge, sweetheart. Anyone can know."

"But I *told* him!"

"Who is he?"

"He dances with us," Gordie said. "He goes with Arthur Grand-court's daughter."

"It wouldn't have happened except for my big mouth!" Tears stung my eyes. "It's all my fault!"

"But, *sweetheart!*" Be reasonable! she means when she says that. But I couldn't. L.G. was still hurting us, and I was the one who let him, and I couldn't stand to have ill spoken of him for everyone to hear.

"What's the matter?" The Senator. Was *everybody* looking at me? I ducked my head so I didn't have to see them.

"The boy got his information from Mad," Mom said quietly.

"Well . . . heck." The Senator sounded puzzled. "It's not like *you've* got anything to be ashamed of! Was that the young whip-persnapper who stood up at the hearing?"

"Yes," Gordie said.

"Bet Arthur Grandcourt isn't too happy!"

"No," Mom said. "It'll make a lot of people angry."

"Can't throw mud without some stickin' to your hands," a quiet voice remarked. Bob. Bob again.

"I wasn't—"

"Not you. Him."

"And every time somebody throws mud at Liz Parker she comes out stronger," the Senator said. "I've seen it time and again. Hey, how about a cold drink while I start the grill!"

* * *

Gam took a long time getting there. Nobody suggested swimming. I saw Gordie and Leslie look at each other once in a while and look at me. Why had I told Neil? Gordie must be wondering. Why Neil, and not him? Why anybody? I sat tracing patterns on my sweating root beer can, listening for Gam.

After a while Mom started talking, and I realized she was telling what had happened to L.G. I listened with a faraway feeling. Mom was letting the story out in the world. She was showing that it had no power to hurt us.

"Wow!" Gordie said. His eyes were wide and serious. "Could *you* do that? If you knew you could save yourself?"

I saw Leslie start to think about it, and then I did, too. Could I? You couldn't drop a little kid once you had hold of her. And you couldn't know you could save yourself, just as you couldn't know that standing there would be your death. It was just unpleasant at first, and then hard, and then . . . but once you started, you couldn't stop.

It was easy for L.G. to run from here because he never saw me, never held me. I'm glad he finally held on to somebody.

"Wow," Gordie said. "I don't know if I could do that!"

At that moment I heard a car slowing far below, turning onto the farm road. I stood up.

In a couple of minutes the car roared into the yard and stopped in a little spray of gravel. I went toward it. My feet felt a long way from my head, uncertain and wavery. The car door opened, and Gam stood up behind it.

She looked three times bigger than normal. The hair seemed to bristle on her head, and her eyes blazed.

"Gam?" I said. "I'm sorry—it was me."

She didn't seem to see me. She barged past, heading toward the group at the grill.

"*Gam!*"

"What, Mad? What?" She looked back impatiently.

"I *told* him! Neil!"

"What? Oh!" She brushed Neil off with the back of her hand.

"Don't give it a second thought!" And she just kept going.

"But—" I stood, gaping at her back. Leslie was sidling toward me. Mom and Bob and Gordie sat motionless in their chairs.

Senator McIver, in his long striped apron, threw a steak sizzling on the grill and looked at Gam, his face unreadable. "They're going for repeal, Liz. Aren't they?"

Gam swelled on a long, slow breath. She said, "Over . . . my . . . *dead* . . . body!"

Mom clapped her hands just once and stopped herself. The Senator's face broke up in a grin that made him look as boyish as Gordie. "Crack this woman a cold one, somebody!"

"I want your phone, Gordon!" Gam said, trampling the end of his sentence. "I've got to call some parade marshals and see how many I can fit in." She was already halfway to the house.

Leslie said, soft enough for only me to hear, "So much for *your* little drama!"

I had to smile. "Yeah. She's got to save the freakin' planet!"

But if I'd truly needed her, if I'd made that plain, she would have stopped. Even in mid-charge she would have stopped. By giving Neil the back of her hand, she'd changed everything. Had she even noticed him?

I didn't think so. In that moment when Tom Corrigan tipped his hand, when the Senator said, "I *knew* it!," Gam's courage rose in that unthinking surge that has always carried her. From that moment on nothing mattered but the fight, and in the fight Neil Bishop wasn't a big gun. He was hardly even a spitball.

"She's not gonna quit," Leslie said. Her eyes were sparkling. "She's just like your father. You know that?"

"No way!"

"Yeah! She's got that new law in her arms, and she thought about dropping it to save herself and get a quiet life, but when it comes right down to it, she *never* would have!"

"Yeah," I said slowly. "Yeah." Something swelled in me then, like a balloon blowing up, and I was smiling, though a little teary, and I felt fine.

24

THERE WERE HORSES in the Barrett parade.

"*You* should have ridden!" Leslie said. "Next year let's come stay for a month and ride in the parade."

"First I have to ride in a show," I said. A parade would be easier, though: no patterns to remember and so many people watching that you couldn't care about them. I wished I'd thought of it.

The Barrett parade was Gam's third. Mom and Bob had dropped her at the start of each parade route, picked her up at the end, driven on to the next town, and now here she was walking with Senator Tom Corrigan and Governor Hessian.

Watching the three of them smile and wave and chat to one another, Leslie said, "You'd never dream they're basically at war."

"I would." Something about Gam's shoulders, something about the way she filled the space and carried her head said aggression to me, said Watch Out!

"Is she lame?" Leslie asked. "Right foot—watch!"

"Yes," I said after a minute.

"Will she be able to dance?"

"If she were Cloud, I wouldn't work her, but she's Gam, so I guess she'll dance."

They passed beyond us, pushed along by the rest of the parade. The tree from the public meeting was there, and Grandcourt Lumber had a big float with trees, loggers using a crosscut saw, builders putting up a house frame. It was a nice float, I had to admit.

Marching bands, more floats, more horses, political groups with signs; a squadron of snowmobilers swarming in complicated patterns on the pavement; a woman on stilts leading the nurses' union marchers; dancers and drummers and fire engines and Model Ts, and suddenly it was over. Main Street remained empty for a minute and then filled with people heading for the booths and food stalls and face painting. The fire department started setting up for the water polo game.

We milled with everyone else. Leslie bought a choker of black nylon filament, made to look like a tattoo. I bought an anklet. "Looks great," Leslie said.

"Yours, too." We wore my denim dresses again, and maybe we walked right past the person who used to own them; who knows?

I avoided Mom and Bob so I wouldn't get introduced to a million of her old friends, but I couldn't avoid introductions entirely. In line at the stuffed-pretzel stall somebody tapped my shoulder. I turned and there was Everett Mouse.

I introduced Leslie, who said, "I've heard about you. You're in one of Mad's dance classes." I gave her a look that said, Don't even *think* of mice, turned away, and there was Morag in her white dress, pushing a man in a wheelchair.

"Madeline!" she said. "I'd like you to meet m'husband, Angus McAe. Angus, this is Liz Parker's granddaughter."

Angus put out his hand, and I took it. His hand was soft and shook a little. His speech was slurred. "Ve'y pleasd meetyou." What a smile, though! His eyes seemed clear and full of a warm light.

But Morag has a husband? In a *wheelchair?*

"We're goin' to go look at the water polo for a while. You make sure your grandmother gets over to the bandstand by—" She broke off, staring past me. "Will y'look at that?"

I turned. Leslie and Everett had stepped out of line. They were holding hands—holding hands!—and he was guiding her through the skip-change of step.

Morag shook her head in a shuddering way. "It'll no be my problem! Phyllis can straighten her out in the fall!" She pushed Angus on through the crowd, and I stared after them. For a moment the world seemed so complex. So much more going on than I'd ever seen: Husbands in wheelchairs. Fathers stuck in the mud, steadfast in the mud. Fathers climbing steeples. Grandmothers who might quit politics or might run for governor, and who knew what more besides? I wanted to see it all. I wanted to plunge right in.

"Thanks," the man ahead of me said, and life was simple again. Herb-and-cheese pretzel, or pesto?

At quarter of two we gathered behind the bandstand, barely able to hear one another as Jerry Grandcourt made announcements. Gordie was already there, looking incredibly handsome in George Marshall's black jacket with the sparkling silver buttons. *Hot*—he looked awfully hot. But gorgeous. Leslie raised one eyebrow at me, and I blushed. "Cut it out!"

Morag fooled around with the music, the Marshalls looked nervous, and Alec looked at his watch. No Sumner yet.

No Neil.

Across the crowded street I spotted Gam. She'd changed into her white dress and was making her way toward us, stopped every few feet by a new knot of people. It was an open question whether she'd make it across the street in fifteen minutes.

"Still lame," Leslie said.

"Mmm." It looked pretty bad, except when she remembered to hide it. "Three parades—my feet would hurt, too!"

But where were Neil and Sumner? I scanned the crowd. There was the Senator, talking with the man who gave all the money to Gam's opponents. The Senator laughed at something the old man said and then shouted, "Liz!" I could hear him over the sound of the crowd, and Gam turned and shouted something back. Faith Hamborough was there, enthroned in a lawn chair, crowned with a big straw hat. Near her were the wheelchair and Angus McAe.

There was Everett, and a good way off were the rest of the Mice. Everett saw me and gave the very slightest of Scottish country dance bows: stiff, from the waist only, highly self-respecting. Oh, I *like* Everett! I thought.

Gam finally joined us, smiling. Under cover of Jerry Grandcourt I asked, "Why are you limping?"

"Blister." She reached for our gillie bag.

"How big?"

She made a circle with thumb and forefinger, the size of a quarter.

"How are you going to dance?" Leslie asked.

Gam shrugged, her smile going a little tight as she pushed her foot into the gillie.

"Here they are!" Morag said. I looked up the street to see Sumner in white dress and tartan sash, making her way through the crowd. As she got closer, I saw that she was frowning.

"Where's Neil?" Morag asked, looking past her.

Sumner flushed, and shook her head. "I don't think he's coming."

"*What?*"

"We—" Sumner closed her lips firmly and lifted her chin, to push back tears or to find the right words. Morag took her by the elbow and drew her closer to the bandstand.

"We came to a parting of the ways," Sumner said at last. She tried to make it sound matter-of-fact, but I could tell it was a struggle. "I couldn't— Senator Parker, I want you to know I had nothing to do with what he said on the radio last night. I thought it was *outrageous!*" The beautiful color glowed in her cheeks, and her eyes flashed. "I told him exactly what I thought of him!"

Gam looked taken aback. "Well, thank you, Sumner. That was . . . good of you."

"Aye," Morag said, "but the timin's a bit unfortunate." She turned. "Madeline! Have y'got your gillies there?"

I clutched the bag. "I—"

"Would you be willin' t'fill in? They're all dances you've done."

"But—" I swallowed. My mouth felt like cotton batting. "I'm— I don't have a white dress!"

"At least y'*have* a dress!"

"But—" Around the corner of the bandstand was a street packed with people, *packed!*

"And coming up in five minutes, Morag McAe's Scottish Country Dance Group," Jerry Grandcourt bellowed. My heart pounded against my chest. I dropped down on the curb and started prying off my sneakers.

Leslie crouched beside me. "*Wow!* Mad, wow!"

"Shh!" I shoved my foot into a gillie. My fingers trembled on the laces. Over my head Morag was shouting up at the bandstand, "Give me *ten* minutes, Jerry! *Ten!* Madeline, you'll dance with Gordie, Liz, dance with Alec, and I'll dance with Sumner as a man—"

Gordie's voice broke in. "First dance is Davy Nick Nack. Cross over and set. Cross back—"

Leslie said, "Oh, look!"

I lifted my head.

Cleaving the crowd, his white ermine sporran jouncing with every stride, came Neil. He wore his black evening jacket and vest, and the buttons glittered, the brilliant July sunshine bounced off the handle of his knife.

"Oh, aye," Morag said. We all waited.

The color was high in Neil's face. His mouth was straight and grim. He must be roasting in that black coat, roasting and humiliated, and maybe even brokenhearted. But as he reached us, he tossed back his wing of blond hair and only said, "Sorry I'm late."

"Hello, Neil." Those were Gam's words. Her voice said more: I know, and you know, that we are not friends, but I, for one, will be perfectly cordial.

Neil went even redder and clenched his jaw hard.

Morag's face was expressionless. "Madeline, looks like we'll no be needin' you."

I felt myself deflate. I looked past them to the street full of people in their shorts and sundresses, their hats, their face paint, all looking toward the empty pavement where the dance would start in a minute. I saw Mom and Bob. His head was exactly level with hers. His handlebar mustache drooped in a mild, melancholy way, and he watched her talk to someone.

Gam turned to Gordie. "All set?"

I stood up beside them. "Give me your sash. I'll take your place."

She looked me in the face, frowning a little. "You don't need to. It's just a blister—"

"I want to."

"Really?"

"Really!" I didn't want to be a watcher anymore. I didn't want to be invisible. I wanted to dance.

Gam's eyes shifted from me to Leslie, and I knew she remembered the dressage show. "All right," she said, and reached up to unpin her sash.

"Liz, what are y'*do*in'?" Morag cried.

"I've got a blister on my foot," Gam said. "Mad's going to step in—"

Morag pounced on her, unfastened the pin at her hip, spun me around. I felt the pin graze my skin as she dug it into my skirt. "I don't care who dances! You or Mad or Jumbo the Clown! But in three minutes we're puttin' a set out there!"

Gam was pinning the sash at my shoulder, and Gordie said urgently, "Cross and set, cross and set. Ones turn by the right and cast—"

The last pin went in. Morag gave my dress a twitch, marshaled us all in a line, and turned to the stand. "Jerry, hit that button!"

Gordie took my hand as the CD player blared a Scottish-sounding "Yankee Doodle." We skipped out into the sunshine, formed a set in front of the bandstand.

My field of vision seemed to widen and deepen. Across from me Gordie with his fabulous nose, his dark, sparkling eyes. Beyond him the faces, all the faces. Mom, gaping. Bob, smiling that slow smile I was starting to like, which pushed up the handlebars of the mustache. All around them, the multicolored crowd.

In denim I must stand out like the dark Lipizzaner, and it didn't matter. It just didn't matter. Above me in line Sumner shook her red hair back, looking indifferent, and across from her Neil's silver buttons glittered, his Adam's apple bobbed, he shifted his shoulders a trifle and took in a deep breath. Cross and set! Gordie mouthed at me. Heat rolled up off the blacktop and beat down on our heads, and here was the first chord.

Bow and curtsy.

Then the fiddles sang, "Davy Davy Nick Nack, Davy Davy Nick Nack—"

Our three skirts lifted and billowed, as if the music were an unseen current floating us off our feet. Across the set the men's kilts swayed. Our three hands reached for the three hands opposite, in perfect unison, and Morag started that little yell, low and private at first, then rising to a wild yip.

"ee-EE-*YEOUGH!*"